ALEATHA ROMIG

NEW YORK TIMES BESTSELLING AUTHOR

ON

THE

EDGE

ON THE EDGE
Stand-alone romantic thriller novel
New York Times, Wall Street Journal, and USA Today
best-selling author

COPYRIGHT AND LICENSE INFORMATION

2022 Edition License

ON THE EDGE

Synopsis:

From New York Times best-selling author Aleatha Romig comes a stand-alone new-adult, romantic thriller where love is new, and monsters lurk in expensive suits behind million-dollar smiles.

Woodland Cliffs Country Club is the crown jewel of the small Monterey-area seaside town. It's comfortable stomping grounds for those born to money and opportunity. With the club's esteemed members from near and far, it's not unusual to spot celebrities, business tycoons, or those with even more power.

It isn't the glamour or intrigue that attracts Rae Watson to seek a summer job at the Cliffs. As a struggling college student, she simply wants to earn money for her senior year at the university and concentrate on classes.

When Rae's friend helps secure her summer employment at the Cliffs, Rae willingly accepts. She quickly learns there's more to the Cliffs, particularly the hidden world of those the country club employs.

The lives of the elite and those who serve them are worlds apart.

What will that mean for Rae and the handsome blue-eyed college student who makes her swoon?

Will she discover the secrets purged from the high cliffs, waiting to be found on the rocky shores, or will she find herself on the edge?

Have you been Aleatha'd?

*ON THE EDGE is a small town, friends-to-lovers, romantic thriller, stand-alone novel.

*Fans of *Downton Abbey* are raving about this modern-day version, in ON THE EDGE.

CHAPTER

1

Bernie Maze

"Hell, it's barely six in the morning," I mumbled, picking up my phone. As soon as I saw the name on the screen, I eased out of the large bed.

Taking one last look at the tangled red hair of the woman still asleep, I adjusted my morning wood, slipped into the attached bathroom, and hit the green button on my phone. Normally, I wouldn't answer calls this early in the morning. There were few exceptions. Seeing the name of the local sheriff before the sun had even breached the horizon was an exception.

My first thought was the redhead.

Would the sheriff be calling about her?

No, she—her name was escaping me—was legal.

Nevertheless, a call from law enforcement had the ability to wake a man in record time.

"Fritz, why the wake-up call?" I asked.

"I need you at Woodland Cliffs right away." He sounded like he was in a wind tunnel or at least outside.

"You caught me asleep." I didn't think admitting such a thing was an egregious error this early in the day. "Can it wait?"

Fritz lowered his volume as the background sounds quieted. "Bernie, I called you as a courtesy. My next call is to Wilma Turner. I suggest you get here first. There's going to be some serious damage control that should probably be in place before she and others are involved."

"Damage control? What happened?"

"We don't have a positive ID yet."

My pulse quickened. "Positive ID?"

"A jogger spotted a body on the beach this morning near four a.m."

"How far from the club? Why is the club involved?" Holding the phone in one hand, I turned on the faucet and splashed cold water on my face. I eyed my tuxedo pants, shirt, and tie from the night before hanging on the hook behind the bathroom door.

"North of Thirteenth Avenue. She was found near the rocks, just beyond the north end of the club's property."

"I still don't know what this has to do with Woodland Cliffs Country Club."

"Like I said, there's not a positive ID. Yet."

Something in his statement made me still. "You know who it is?"

"Yeah, get down here now."

"I'm on my way." I pushed disconnect and pulled last night's attire from the hook. There wasn't time to go home and get clean clothes. I'd blame it on the late night if anyone asked.

A few minutes later, I stepped back into the hotel room, searching for my shoes and tuxedo jacket. Light from the dawn peeked around the drapes, giving me just enough illumination to locate my missing items.

"Bernie?" the redhead asked groggily, lifting her head from the pillow. "Where are you going?"

I walked to the bed and laid a kiss on her hair. "I received an unexpected call."

She turned, pulling the sheet over her breasts.

For only a moment, I thought about the way those firm round beauties bounced when I was balls deep in her tight—

I didn't have time to reminisce.

If I did, my morning wood that had disappeared during my talk with the sheriff would come back with a vengeance. Walking toward the door, I pulled out my wallet and laid a fifty-dollar bill on the small round table near the window. "Sorry, sweetie, you'll need to get breakfast by yourself."

Her green eyes narrowed. "Don't do that. I'm not a whore."

No, she wasn't. She was an employee at the

country club I oversaw. "Consider it a donation to the education fund." I lifted a finger to my lips. "Remember, this—what happened—isn't for general knowledge."

Her grin grew. "I have a friend, one who could use a job."

Of course she did.

Someday I'd learn to stop banging the help, but as long as they were twenty to twenty-two with perky breasts and tight pussies, I wasn't sure when that day would come. "Talk to Max." He was in charge of the kitchen and dining areas.

"May I tell him you sent me?"

"No. But if he doesn't help you out, let me know."

"Thanks, Bernie." She smiled. "I had fun."

"Mr. Maze."

She nodded. "Yeah, right, Mr. Maze."

Even though I couldn't come up with this redheaded beauty's name to save my soul, the next time she saw me would most likely be at the club. Few on the payroll were given liberty to address me by my first name in that setting, even those who had left their lipstick on my cock.

Despite wearing last night's formal wear, I lifted my chin to the morning breeze. Technically, I was in Orange Grove, a small community outside of Woodland. The hotels were cheaper here, and their staff asked fewer questions. In only minutes, I'd be back to Woodland, a seaside community bordering the more well-known Monterey, California. Woodland was the perfect community for its filthy rich residents and visitors. Golf courses, pickleball courts, tennis courts, pools, and beaches covered as much real estate as homes. And along that prestigious shoreline was Woodland Cliffs Country Club.

I slipped behind the steering wheel of my Tesla Model X, the girl I'd left behind in the hotel room a distant memory. My concern was what, or more accurately who, was waiting on the beach. My thoughts went back to when I left the club last night. It had been after two a.m.

I'd stayed for the Harvest Gathering, one of our annual events that brought our most valued VIPs to the club. A majority of our members were local Northern California residents; however, events such as last night's attracted out-of-town members. We had high-spending clientele from across the country and even a few from overseas.

For many of them, it was a reunion of sorts. Adelaide Montague and Oren Demetri, for example, arrived from London to spend some time with their family, Lennox Demetri and his wife, Alexandria. Both couples had become members years ago, after Lennox and Alexandria's marriage. Alexandria was the one who had recommended Woodland Cliffs. She had fond memories of the West Coast while attending Stanford in Palo Alto and liked having the connection, even if they rarely visited and their annual membership cost more than some families of four grossed in a year.

To be honest, those were the members I appreciated—the ones who rarely graced our doors. They were much easier to please.

Since Fritz believed this woman was connected to the club, my thoughts went to our executive board. There were the Turners, of course. They were a founding family. Wilma, the matriarch, was private and carried herself with a regal air. According to *Forbes*, she had every right to do so. Her children and grandchildren weren't as socially aware. It seemed to be the expected result of being raised as they'd no doubt been.

Then there were also the Cannons, Holmeses, Olivers, Harrises, Hamiltons, and Bowens—all people with enough money to make them powerful. No one liked bad publicity. My thoughts flipped through our membership books as I pulled along Scenic Boulevard near Thirteenth Street, parking behind Sheriff Strong's car. He wasn't alone. More law enforcement officers had arrived, keeping the early risers away from the scene below.

Fritz met me at the crest of the hill. "We're trying to clear the scene."

I nodded, peering around him to the beach below. Near a group of EMTs, I saw a body bag on a stretcher. Even the thought of a body spending too much time in the cold salt water made my stomach turn. "Who is it, Fritz?"

"I'd like you to take a look."

It was a good thing I hadn't had time for breakfast or even coffee. As the EMT pulled down the zipper and the bloated face and blond hair came into view, I knew who the victim was. "Fuck, she was at the club last night."

Fritz nodded. "Ellen Temple."

He didn't ask; he knew, the same as I did. "Yeah."

"Did you see her leave?"

I tried to recall. "There were a lot of members last night for the Harvest Gathering. It's an annual thing, you know."

"One of the EMTs said there was a call a few weeks back to Henri Turner's house."

I shook my head. "I really shouldn't be told—"

"Was she with Henri last night?" Fritz asked.

I inhaled. "Let me know when I need to give a statement. Until then..."

He nodded. "I get it, but damn, this could finally be it."

It as in the time Henri Turner might finally be caught at something.

The Turners were too influential in Woodland—hell, in California, the country, and the world—for someone like me to point a finger at any one of them.

As Fritz zipped the bag over Ellen's face, I shook my head. "Damn is right."

CHAPTER

2

Rae Watson

Early May the following year

"Now that classes are done for the semester,"
Robyn said, "what are your plans?"

I lifted my face to the clear, sun-filled
sky and sighed. "I just found out I have a new job."

"Tired of the grocery store?"

"Tired of the hours," I said. "Not that the new job
will be better as far as late nights, but no early mornings means I can get some sleep."

Robyn nodded as we walked to our cars. When
we'd met before our freshman year, we both
noticed our resemblance and joked that it was like
the old Disney movie where two girls meet at camp
and discover they're twin sisters. Our resemblance
wasn't quite that strong, but our height, body
shape, and coloring were all similar. Since I was

from Ohio and Robyn was from California, we ruled out the twin possibility. Even so, we became friends.

"Keep in touch." She nudged me with her elbow. "Let me know if anything happens between you and Frankie."

A genuine smile curled my lips as I imagined Frankie's smile and blue eyes. "Frankie is a flirt. He has been since the beginning of the year." Shaking my head, I straightened my shoulders. "Besides, I'm not looking for a guy. I have one more year of school, and then the sky's the limit. I don't need some relationship holding me back."

"There are perks to a relationship."

We reached our cars. I leaned against mine and grinned. "Yes, you've been sharing your perks or more specifically, sexual exploits, for the last semester. What are you going to do with Parker all the way down in Long Beach for a few months?"

Robyn tilted her head and grinned. "I'm going with him."

"To his parents'?"

"His aunt and uncle are going on a six-week tour of Europe and asked if he'd stay at their house."

"Wow."

"Yeah, I can't believe it. They have two dogs, so the real job is watching the dogs."

"Are they all right with him bringing you?"

"I'm not sure he's asked," she admitted, leaning

against her white Chevy Sonic. "I don't care. Six weeks of playing house is worth quitting my job."

I felt the disappointment Robyn wasn't showing. "But you loved working at the day care."

"They'll hire me back next year, or they won't." She shrugged. "Let me know about your new job, and I can apply there."

"I'll definitely keep you posted. I've been told that they only hire with recommendations. If I'm still there in the autumn, I'll be glad to give you one."

"Who recommended you?"

"Beth," I said as I unlocked the door to my car.

Robyn's face paled. "She works at Woodland Cliffs."

"That's my new job."

"What about the killer on the loose?"

"You watch too many crime shows. The sheriff's department closed the case, calling it accidental. Too much alcohol and she slipped."

"And no one saw it happen or reported her missing."

I shook my head. "Go have fun in Long Beach. I'll be making so much in tips, I won't have to work during our final semester and can concentrate on classes."

Robyn smiled. "No tips for me, but plenty of sex."

The traffic was picking up. After living in the Monterey area for three years, I was used to the influx of seasonal residents that came with the spring and summer months. This year, I looked at each fancy car a bit differently. Maybe Mr. Mercedes over there was a member of Woodland Cliffs. Or Miss Tesla. Beth said servers had to tip share with the rest of the kitchen. My entry position would be bussing tables. After the years I'd waitressed, I was confident I'd make my way up to server by the end of the summer.

I pulled my six-year-old Honda up to the outdoor farmers market.

With the din of customers and the spring breeze blowing my hair, my attention was on the produce. Cutting corners was a way of life for a broke college student, but that didn't always include cheap junk food. I lifted a tomato from the stand.

"If you squeeze it, you can tell if it's ready."

I turned to the familiar voice. My smile grew at the sight of the very person Robyn had mentioned. "Hi, Frankie. Ready for what?"

His light-blue eyes sparkled in the sunshine. It was true that he was a flirt, but that didn't mean he wasn't good at it, that his smile didn't melt my insides or that his wide shoulders and long legs didn't catch my attention.

"Ready to explode in your mouth."

My eyes widened as his laugh filled the air. "You're getting the visual, aren't you?"

I shook my head. The visual wasn't of a tomato.

He took a step closer. "Rae, I've been trying to ask you out for the last year."

"Really?" I asked. "I never heard the question."

"Because I didn't want you to turn me down."

"And you think I will?"

"I'm hoping you won't."

I pursed my lips as I felt my cheeks rise. "I know how you can find out...if I'll accept or turn you down."

Frankie took a deep breath, his chest inflating. "Will you go to dinner with me?"

"You went big. Not coffee or studying. Dinner."

"Go big or go home, I always say. Classes are over, and I want to spend more time with you than coffee."

My grin grew. "Sure," I said, happy he had asked. "I'd like to go to dinner with you."

He let out his breath. "Are you still living where we worked on that project for economics?"

"Yes."

"I can pick you up at seven."

"I would rather meet you."

Frankie shook his head. "I'm not a stranger you met at the market." He tilted his head and grinned. "The ride is part of the date."

"Where are we going?"

"You'll find out." He turned toward his motorcycle. "Wear jeans and bring a jacket."

My eyes widened. "We're not taking your bike, are we?" It was all I'd ever seen Frankie drive, but surely there was a car somewhere.

"Yes, Rae. Tonight, I'll show you the stars."

The stars.

As I gathered my groceries, an unfamiliar sense of

anticipation took hold within me. Such as a seed finally letting its shell crack, as roots broke free and a sprout sought sunshine. I wasn't sure where this would lead with Frankie. I only knew that I was excited something was finally beginning.

CHAPTER

3

Rae

L ater that evening with the wind blowing in my face, I leaned against Frankie's back as we drove south along Highway 1. I'd never been on a motorcycle before, and when Frankie showed up at my apartment, I admit I tried talking him into driving my car.

The sun moved lower to the horizon as we wound along the scenic highway, until we finally stopped on the dirt shoulder next to the road. From where we were, there was a steep decline to a sandy beach below. "Where are we?"

"Garrapata State Park. When I was young, my grandpa would bring me here." Frankie leaned the bike to the side as I slipped off.

The solid ground beneath my boots was welcome. As I took off the helmet, the wind blew my light-colored hair and I took in the view. "It's beautiful."

"Wait until the sun goes down."

Frankie opened one of the saddlebags and pulled out two cloth bags. "Our dinner."

"This is where we're going? No restaurant?"

"It's better than a restaurant." He opened the second saddlebag and pulled out a beach blanket. "Come with me, Rae, and see the stars."

I followed a step behind as we climbed down a wooden staircase. The hills around us were covered in clusters of flowers, yellow, orange, and purple too. About halfway down, I turned around and looked up the mountain. "You know, going down means going back up."

Frankie laughed. "No wonder you're number two in the class."

"Are you making fun of me?"

He looked back over his broad shoulder, his light-blue eyes shining. "Only a little. You see, I'm fucking impressed with the way you handled macro- and microeconomics. I don't have a problem admitting you're smarter than me." He shrugged. "I finally have you to myself. So I think that makes me smart too."

Once on the beach, Frankie laid the blanket out on the sand and kicked off his boots and socks. "Take off your shoes. It's easier to climb the rocks."

After I did, he offered me his hand. "Come with me before the sun sets."

I looked in all directions, out across the glistening

waves, up the staircase, and over at the land jutting out to the water. "Where are all the other people?"

"Even when I was a kid, this place was usually deserted."

With my hand in his, Frankie led me up onto large rocks. In nooks and crevasses were small tide pools. At low tide, the pools were alive with colorful inhabitants—starfish, snails, and sponges. Abalone glistened with different hues as the sun lowered. From high above the surf, the view seemed to go on forever.

"This is amazing," I said, crouching down and inspecting the colorful sea anemones.

"Don't touch them."

I pulled my hand back. When I looked up, Frankie was smiling. "Are you teasing me? They look like flowers."

He shrugged. "I'm not. They can sting. I mean, they won't kill you, but I'd rather our first date not result in a visit to the emergency room."

"Our first date?"

Frankie offered me his hand. "Come on. We have dinner waiting."

Before the sun reached the horizon, we were back at the blanket. Frankie pulled a bottle of wine from one of the bags. "You're old enough, right?"

"I turn twenty-one next week."

Using a wine opener, he popped the cork. After pouring a small amount into a tumbler, he handed it my direction. "I've always taken you for a rule breaker."

I took the tumbler. "Really?"

"Only a little." He filled his tumbler and lifted it to mine. "Cheers, Rae. To our first dinner."

Our tumblers clinked. I lifted the rim to my lips and tasted the rosé. It was sweeter than I expected. "I like this."

"My mom always says this one is a good starter wine."

"Your mom likes wine?"

"It's kind of what my family does."

"They work in a winery?"

Frankie smiled and turned toward the setting sun. "Something like that. Thanks for coming out with me." As he pulled our meal from the second bag, he asked, "What are your summer plans?"

"Working."

He nodded. "Yeah, me too." I was about to ask where, when he said, "Maybe we can see each other again."

The jury was still out on a commitment, but so far, I was enjoying our evening.

"You saved me tonight," he said, handing me something wrapped in paper. "I hope you like chicken salad."

"I do. Chicken salad is good." I started freeing the sandwich from the paper. "How did I save you?"

"Dinner with the family." He leaned back, lifting

his handsome face to the darkening sky. "Here with you is much better than the Cliffs."

My appetite disappeared. "The Cliffs, as in the country club?"

"Yeah, it's not all that great, but maybe I can take you there one day. The pools are crowded but nice."

"You're a member?"

CHAPTER

4

Rae

One week later

The swinging door closed behind me as I carried an armful of plates, with two glasses wobbling precariously on the top of the load. With my attention on what I was carrying, I narrowly missed a collision with another server.

"Watch it, newbie," he said.

By the time I looked up, all I saw was the back of the guy's head, his wide shoulders covered in the standard country club embroidered white shirt, and his nice ass also covered in the typical black pants. That would be typical for guys. My blouse was standard, in the tapered feminine cut, and instead of black pants I was wearing a black pencil skirt.

Making my way to the dish line, I lowered the plates onto the conveyor belt.

"Don't forget the glasses."

Before the dishes disappeared behind a rubbery curtain, I reached for the two glasses and moved them to the large dishwasher container already mostly full. For only a brief second, I considered how many of those containers were filled each day, between the drinks served during the day at the pool, terrace, within the VIP-only locations, and the drinks served in the evening at the bar and restaurant. For an exclusive club that boasted a very limited membership, I'd guess hundreds of drinks and hundreds of containers full of glasses.

When I turned away from the glasses, my gaze met that of my friend Beth. Although we were wearing the same outfit, her petite form, bright red hair, and green eyes looked nothing like my five foot six, blond hair, and light-brown eyes. "Thank you," I said, letting out a long sigh. "How much do these people drink?"

A grin curled her lips. "If you mean liquid, a lot. The fruit bars near the tennis and pickleball courts go through cases of water a day."

"I meant...*drink*."

"A lot." Her voice lowered. "I guess when top-shelf liquor is at your fingertips, and a driver is waiting in the parking lot, there's no limit to the amount of alcohol one can consume."

Driver?

I hadn't even considered that there were drivers. My head shook. This was a whole new world for me.

For a second, I thought about Frankie. We'd now been out twice, the beach and a restaurant for my birthday. Even so, I hadn't had the guts to tell him where I was working. Thankfully, I hadn't spotted him in the dining room.

This might be a world he was used to, but to me, it was as if I'd entered a foreign country or maybe a new planet.

"It takes some getting used to," she said.

"I feel so out of place."

Beth reached out and squeezed my arm. "You're doing great."

"I don't feel like it." I stepped to the side, clearing the way for other employees of Woodland Cliffs Country Club to deposit their loads of partially empty plates, silverware, and glasses. "I thought this would be like waitressing, but it's not."

Beth looked at the clock located over the swinging door. For a fancy place like this, the clock was plain, reminding me of the ones in the classrooms of every school I ever attended.

"Less than two hours and we're off," she said. "Once we clock out, come with me, and I'll show you where we Muggles like to unwind."

"Muggles?"

"You know," she said in a whisper, "those people without the power of—"

"Magic?"

"Money."

21

I'd known Beth for two years. We'd met in a second-year speech class at a nearby community college, where we'd both completed enough hours to transfer to California State University. We'd been paired for a mock debate and hit it off right away. One of our connections was our constant search for income. That search was what brought me to Woodland Cliffs. Beth had worked here for the last two summers, and last year, she'd stayed on during the off-season.

I wasn't completely certain these posh towns in Northern California had an off-season. Compared to where I'd grown up in Ohio, the seasons here consisted of one, two if you included the rainy season, and three if fire season came into the mix. Thankfully, the fire season hadn't reared its ugly head to a serious degree since I'd moved to this area.

Beth vouching for me was the reason I was here tonight in the Woodland Cliff's attire and the most uncomfortable heels I'd ever worn.

"Do you mean you have a party spot that you've been keeping from me?"

She shrugged. "It's a private area on Woodland property. It's off-limits to the members and non-members. When we get there, you'll know why."

"Oh, I'm intrigued."

"Watson, members are waiting," Mr. Kluser, the kitchen manager, said with a nod to the dining room. He turned Beth's way. "You too."

Was it my overactive imagination, or did his voice slow when he spoke to Beth?

The answer didn't matter. I needed to listen. Getting fired on my first night wasn't my plan.

Beth and I both nodded and made our way back onto the dining room floor.

I stopped over the threshold and took in the sheer opulence. In a way, simply being here, on the premises, took my breath away. It was the feeling of a fish out of water or a peasant in a castle.

The dining room was something out of a storybook or maybe a movie. From the floor-to-ceiling windows with a spectacular view of the now-dark Pacific Ocean, to the ornate, glistening light fixtures, the starched linen tablecloths, and the numerous bouquets of fresh flowers, it was spectacular.

I'd had that thought when I had entered the dining area for the first time for my interview. To me, simply entering the grounds was intimidating.

That didn't seem to be the way the members saw it.

Their indifference was clear not only in their mannerisms and gestures but their attitudes.

Thankfully, at nearly ten at night, those members present had drastically decreased. Even on a Friday night, the kitchen stopped serving meals for the dining room at ten o'clock. Drinks and desserts were served until ten thirty. After that, it was our job to clean. Of course, if a member decided to sit at a table until eleven or midnight, we were on standby. I hadn't participated in the mad dash for cleanup yet, but I had heard stories.

The main dining room where I was working bussing tables was only one area of the club. There were private dining rooms with assigned themes, a gentlemen's suite called the Tertian Lounge, with cigars and top-shelf liquor, and also a ladies' suite. It was a deck with a sensational view of the Pacific Ocean, a private bar, and reportedly the best martinis on the planet.

According to Beth, I might be asked to work the gentlemen's room on occasion—it was a very lucrative and coveted assignment. Openings were rare, but if offered, she recommended I take it.

The ladies' deck would never be on my time card. Those positions were held by people like the guy with curly dark hair and the nice ass. Yes, I admitted the entire establishment was sexist. The stupid two-inch black heels and tight skirt were further examples.

The establishment also paid well, and with my current financial status and one more year of college, I chose to tuck away my modern beliefs and paste a smile on my face as long as I wore the sexist attire.

One day, I'd be able to afford to have my ideals.

Today wasn't that day.

"Table seventeen," Mr. Kluser said as he stepped through the swinging door, back onto the dining room floor.

The way he stood, arms crossed and watching

everything, sent a cold chill over my skin despite the perspiration I'd worked up throughout my shift. It was as if he could see and hear everything—a drill sergeant in a suit instead of a uniform.

Mr. Kluser tapped my shoulder and tilted his head toward the long table by the windows. "Learn the numbers, kid."

CHAPTER

5

Rae

id.

K Despite the rise of the small hairs on the back of my neck, my attention went to my task at hand as Mr. Kluser's one word reverberated through my thoughts. At officially twenty-one years old, I didn't consider myself a kid.

Hell, I'd lived through more than most of the people seated in the dining room. While I didn't know that for sure, it was an easy assumption that their lives had been a cakewalk compared to mine and others like me.

Mr. Kluser's stare narrowed.

"Thanks," I mumbled as I walked to table seventeen.

With my feet aching, I scanned the disaster zone. Usually glasses and dishes were taken away throughout the night. However, the party who had sat at this table demanded that only one server work with them. No one else was to approach the table until they were gone.

Beth came up beside me. "We'll all help."

I looked around. "No, you have other things to do."

"It'll go faster, and besides, none of us leave until we all do."

"Hey, newbie" —the voice belonged to the guy I'd almost run into earlier— "welcome to the twilight zone."

"Sorry about our almost collision," I said a bit bashfully. While his shoulders and ass had been on my radar earlier, now that he was looking down at me, it was his hazel eyes, near-perfect smile, and easy expression that captured my attention.

Mr. Good-Looking grinned. "Beth talked you up. Rae, right?"

I tried to pick up a fifth glass. "Yes." I peered up at him. "And you're...?" Mr. Good-Looking wouldn't be a good way to address him.

"Chad."

I wasn't sure why, but his name made me laugh. "I imagined a Chad with sun-bleached blond hair and a surfboard."

"Everyone needs a goal. That's mine."

As we entered the kitchen and deposited our loads into the gray container and onto the conveyor belt, I asked, "Did I see you waiting on that table? Were you the server?"

"Yeah. Mrs. Turner likes me."

"Oh?" I waggled my eyebrows.

He did a quick shake of his head. "You might have noticed her. She was the white-haired lady at the head of the table."

A giggle bubbled in my throat. "Oh, so not *oh*."

"No."

"Why didn't they want anyone else to be near them?"

His eyes opened wide. As they did, gold flecks swirled with other shades. Green and turquoise mixed around his growing pupil.

"Are you serious?" he asked.

Mr. Kluser cleared his throat.

I turned toward the swinging door, headed back to the big table, Chad at my side. The club had a policy against using serving trays or busser buckets or any type of container while clearing tables. It was believed that Woodland Cliffs was better than that. Using common containers was tacky. As blisters formed on top of the blisters already growing on my feet, I thought tacky sounded...nice.

Of course, my opinion didn't exactly match the country-club set. Growing up, I was someone who was excited to go to Applebee's for special occasions. Maybe I didn't understand the finer points of Northern California living.

As Chad and I both reached for more dishes, I said, "I was serious. What don't I know?"

"Newbie, if you're working here, you need to learn names and learn them fast. First, the Turners are some of the wealthiest members of the club." He lowered his voice. "Top fifty on *Forbes* wealthiest list last year. Mrs. Turner and her late husband were founding members of this club. And what she wants, she gets."

I tried to think of the name. "Broadcasting?"

"No, that's a different family. Think wealthier." He grinned. "They made their fortune the old-fashioned way."

Prostitution.

I wasn't sure why that was my first thought. "The old-fashioned way?"

"They inherited it."

Working together, we soon had the Turners' table and others down to the tablecloth. In and out of the kitchen, we tried to appear busy. With each passing minute, my eyelids fought their desire to close. If it weren't for the pain in my feet, they might have won.

Eventually, the last table with diners emptied.

Without warning, the entire staff went into hypermode. It was different than I'd imagined. First, after Mr. Kluser shut the dining room entrance, all the women kicked off their shoes into one corner. Literally, in this fancy dining room, there was a huge pile of identical black patent-leather heels.

"Do it," Beth said, wiggling her toes. "It feels great."

I'd spent forty dollars on my shoes. "How do I know I'll get mine back?"

"Didn't you write your name on the soles?"

When I hesitated, she nudged me. "Maybe I forgot that bit of information. Kick yours to the side. Tomorrow, have your name on them. Come on. Our best record is twenty-six minutes and forty-four seconds. If we beat that, we all get a shot from the bar."

"Seriously?"

The dining room was a flurry of centerpieces and tablecloths. As each table was stripped down to the tabletop, it was cleaned, dried, and covered again with a fresh tablecloth. Other people emptied the vases. Perfectly beautiful fresh flowers were discarded into large trash bags and empty vases placed back where they belonged.

"Tomorrow," Beth explained, "before the dining room opens for lunch, the florist brings all new flowers."

I frowned at the trash bags filled with flowers. "Isn't there some place to donate them?"

Beth's lips formed a straight line. "Not your battle, Goldilocks."

I sighed. Beth was the only one in California who knew the nickname my father gave me as a child. Simply hearing it made things better.

All at once, everyone came to a stop and turned toward the kitchen.

Mr. Kluser stepped away from the wall. "Very close. Twenty-seven minutes and seven seconds."

The room filled with a deep sigh.

He looked in my direction. "Maybe once Miss Watson learns the ropes, you'll beat your record."

CHAPTER

6

Rae

M r. Kluser's remark hung in the air. "Maybe once Miss Watson learns the ropes, you'll beat your record."

Nice way to be called out.

As more murmurs filled the room, uncomfortable warmth covered my skin, from my breasts up my neck until it filled my cheeks. Swallowing, I looked at the man who had turned the spotlight on me. He was staring my way, but not in a way for our eyes to meet. No, his gaze unapologetically scanned from my head to my toes. Finally, he spoke, "Don't sweat it, Watson. Scarlett's shoes are tough to fill." With that, Mr. Kluser turned and walked back into the kitchen.

"You did great," Beth said as the women made their way to the large pile of shoes.

"It just means you get to buy us all a round," a brunette said.

I'd seen her working. She was a server, not a busser like me. I'd been a waitress since high school, but according to the club's rules, everyone had to work their way up the ladder. From where I stood on the bottom rung, there were a lot of people ahead of me.

I shrugged. Working at Woodland Cliffs wasn't my goal. Since the bottom rung here was also the bottom rung on my real ladder to success, I could endure a summer. One more year of college and things would change.

Beth reached for my elbow. "Now, come with me, and I'll show you how we unwind."

With my shoes in my hand, I whispered, "He gives me a weird feeling."

"He?"

"Mr. Kluser." I shivered.

Beth shrugged. "That's just Max."

Max?

She knew his first name.

"Will he be where we unwind?" I asked.

"Oh, no."

"So he's not a Muggle?"

Beth did a quick shake of her head. "He is. He just won't admit it."

As we walked with the others toward the locker room, I asked, "Who is Scarlett?"

"She worked here last year."

"Did she find a better job?"

"No one knows," Beth said as she opened her

locker. "She worked through the autumn season, and one day, she was gone."

"Is she all right?"

"She sent an email saying she was quitting." Beth shrugged. "You know, California is the land of opportunities and dreams. I hope hers came true."

The locker room was located behind the kitchen. It was a large room that looked as though, in an earlier life, it had been a warehouse or maybe a storage room. Voices echoed from the cement floor into the open rafters as I took in the rows of lockers. A woman named Jean had assigned me mine after my interview. None of the lockers actually locked.

She promised there wasn't a problem with theft.

As I moved the latch and opened the door, I half expected to see my things gone. I reached up to the shelf for the most expensive possession within, my phone. Relief filled me as I lifted it from the shelf.

Jean had also shown me the attached bathroom. There were two. One for the guys, and the other for the girls. Our bathroom had sinks, mirrors, stalls, and showers. I could only assume the guys' was similar. We all shared the unisex locker room.

Beth pursed her lips and threw her phone back on the shelf in her locker.

"Is everything okay?" I asked.

"Yeah, it was nothing." Forcing a grin, Beth unbuttoned and unzipped her skirt. Quickly, it dropped to her ankles, and she slipped a pair of shorts over her lace panties. My eyes went in all directions as guys and girls were doing the same thing, stripping from their club uniforms and donning more casual and comfortable clothes.

"Hurry," Beth said, wiggling her toes into her sandals. "Once we leave our uniforms for laundry, we're out of here."

With a shake of my head, I quickly shed my work clothes and slipped on the cotton sundress and sandals I'd worn to the club. I grabbed the light sweater I'd brought along for after the sun went down. Northern California wasn't nearly as warm as where I'd grown up; however, it had much steadier temperatures. In Akron, we could boast minus ten degrees in the winter and ninety in the summer.

Nevertheless, this was early June, and I liked sundresses.

"Hey, newbie," Chad said, "if Beth didn't invite you to our standing after-work party, I will."

"She did," I said with a grin.

"Stop at the liquor store. You owe us," the brunette from earlier said.

"Um, is there one close?" I asked, while simultaneously wondering if I had enough money.

My response earned a laugh from not only the brunette, but everyone within earshot.

A few minutes later, Beth warned, "First, don't worry about McKenzie. She's pulling your chain." My friend leaned closer. "Listen, Chad's nice enough, but watch yourself."

"Watch myself."

"Yeah, I think that in the time I've been here, he's bagged every new girl. It's a contest for him."

I wanted to ask if she was one of them but decided against it.

My lips came together. Chad was cute, but the last thing I needed in life was to be a notch on some guy's belt, especially a guy whose life goal was to be a bleached-blond surfer. "I'm kind of seeing someone."

"You are?" Beth came closer. "Why haven't you told me?"

"It's nothing." And after taking this job, if he saw me working here, it was probably history.

What rich guy who belongs to a country club wants to date the help?

Yes, going out with the other servers—those like me —was a good plan.

The weariness I'd felt a few hours ago disappeared as I followed along. We all traipsed through a wooded area, slipped around a gate, and found ourselves on a narrow cliff.

My feet came to a stop as I stared down at the moonlit sandy beach probably twenty feet below. "Holy shit."

Beth grinned. "See, no members here. With the bigwig attorneys those people employ, this area was a lawsuit waiting to happen."

"Was?"

"You heard about her, Ellen Temple?"

"The lady who died?"

Beth nodded. "They think she wandered down here. That's the story, but it's not true."

"How do you know?"

"Because we were here."

I took one more look down the trail. Unlike the steps at the park, this was more rugged. "What if one of us falls?"

"They hire someone to replace us," McKenzie said as she passed me and made her way down the steep trail.

Chad lifted his palm when I stepped closer to the trail. "Watch your step," he said as the moonlight reflected in his hazel eyes.

"I'm good," I answered, keeping my hand away from his.

Once we reached the bottom, Chad reached into the pocket of his shorts and pulled out a slightly smashed flower.

"For me?" I asked as a smile formed.

"You looked sad they were being thrown away."

Taking in his grin, I reached for the flower.

"Tell me why Beth called you Goldilocks."

CHAPTER

7

Henri Turner

"**Y**our mother, sir," Richard said, handing me a phone as I entered my kitchen from the garage.

"I'm not home."

Richard was my personal attendant, butler, manservant, and jack-of-all-trades. Fate had been kind to bring us together. Many years ago, I helped him out of a financial and legal dilemma. From that moment forward, his loyalty was unbreakable.

A few years younger than me, Richard Reynolds was physically fit. He kept his dark hair short and tight. It reminded him of his military days. There wasn't a task that I hesitated to pass his way. He'd never refused a request.

Of all the tasks I'd asked him to undertake, it was humorous that speaking to my mother was the thing that caused his brow to furrow. Richard hit a button on the telephone. "I'm sorry, Mrs. Turner. It was my mistake. I heard the cook. Mr. Turner hasn't arrived home yet." He paused as he took a deep breath. "Yes, ma'am. I will tell him as soon as he arrives." After a moment, he hit disconnect and exhaled. "She said she's been trying to reach you since you left the country club." He nodded. "She's concerned."

My temples throbbed as I went to the liquor cabinet and poured myself two fingers of bourbon. After swirling the amber liquid, I lifted the tumbler to my lips and emptied the glass. With newfound energy, I turned back to Richard. "Sorry to put it on you, man. Call her back in fifteen minutes. Let her know I arrived home safely. I'm occupied with a call I received on my way home, and I'll call her in the morning."

"A call?" He undoubtedly saw that I wasn't on a call.

"Or you could tell her the truth, but I doubt she wants to hear that."

Richard nodded. "A call." A grin came to his lips. "Overseas? At this time of night, I'd suspect it was from London."

"Make it Dubai. I've been working with a broker over there for years."

"Yes, sir. Dubai."

The lights from the kitchen faded as I walked through the dining room, living room, and sitting room. This house was too big for one man. Of course, I hadn't thought that when I'd bought it, back when I had prospects of a storybook marriage.

I stopped at the bottom of the large staircase and peered upward into the darkened landing. Six bedrooms in this market would mean I could sell this monstrosity and make a killing. With two master suites, a theater room, an exercise room, and a fucking infinity pool, it was everything Ellen wanted. And now, it echoed like a clanging gong in an empty bell tower.

Hell, if I sold, I could put the money toward a bigger boat, one that would allow me to sail away from this city, the family businesses, and the memories. The twisting in my chest told me that would never happen.

There was an undeniable perk to a barely inhabited huge home—seclusion.

Reaching the top of the stairs, I went right instead of left.

My suite was to the left.

Nothing called to me from my suite. Oh, it had amenities: a fully stocked liquor cabinet, a television the size of a parking space, a large, lonely bed, and a balcony that allowed me to listen to the ocean as I drifted off to sleep. None of those things would give me what I sought.

I knew what had me worked up. It was the damn country club and that young man, Chad.

As I'd driven home, I decided to talk to Bernie Maze. As chief financial officer of the country club, he'd listen to me. I'd tell him that Chad needed to go. I would tell him that my mother believed he'd stolen from her. Jewelry or cash. I'd work on the story. Of course, I'd have to tell him that my mother was too upset and disappointed in the young man to bring about the charges herself. She would remain quiet as long as the server was let go.

I wasn't certain how Chad had any knowledge of what I'd done, but every time he looked at me or spoke to me, I felt it—the accusation, the judgment, and the superiority condemnation. I didn't need shit from some two-bit server. Legend had me listed as one of Woodland's most eligible bachelors. I could have a date with any one of the women in that dining room tonight, even most of the married ones, if I wanted.

I'd tried the traditional route with Ellen.

That required the right relationship, one she and I didn't have. Now, I was back to what I knew could bring me relief, satisfaction, and the edge I needed. I'd been here before with others. It wasn't a relationship that could be maintained indefinitely. If history was a good indicator, what we had would probably not end well. Nevertheless, we'd put too much time into our agreement with Scarlett to walk away just yet.

Besides, walking was only an option for me.

The locks clicked as I unlocked the door to the rarely used corridor. Well-greased hinges gave no warning as I pushed the door inward. The hallway beyond was equally dark. I didn't need light. Even though I hadn't been down this way in over three days, I could find my way here with my eyes closed.

No one entered this area except Richard and me.

To the rest of the staff, those who came and went from the property, it was empty, a solemn reminder of what I didn't want to recall. It only took one warning from Richard to keep curious eyes and ears away. The additional insulation did a wonderful job of containing sound.

Removing my cuff links and placing them in my pocket, I rolled up each sleeve, took a deep breath, and savored the bourbon coursing through my veins. As I inserted the key into the dead bolt, my circulation roared to life. It was a jolt of energy replenishing what I'd lost at that boring family gathering. The electricity surged as I anticipated what was beyond this door.

Scarlett didn't know when I'd show. I found it best to keep her waiting and ready. After all, that was now her job, her life—to be at my beck and call. There may not be the public approval of a beautiful and intelligent woman on my arm as I'd had with Ellen, but there was definitely something to be said for the benefits that only happened in private.

I had a name to uphold, a standing in the community. My elder brother, Harry, had gotten wind regarding some of my preferences. It was an uncomfortable confrontation. And still it turned out better than it could have. The information he'd thought was significant was merely the tip of the proverbial iceberg.

Harry agreed to keep my secret as long as I vowed not to let what was private become public.

"Don't end up on social media, Henri. It would kill Mother. Find a way to do what you want, without public knowledge."

I doubted my brother meant for me to take my own private companion—a sex toy—but in all fairness, he wasn't very specific. And although I had a history of such possessions, in the beginning, my relationship with Scarlett wasn't intended to culminate into what it was today. One thing led to another. She fit the bill.

Scarlett understood my needs, better than Ellen.

And then Scarlett made a costly mistake.

Perhaps what she'd said was uttered in jest.

Scarlett insinuated that if she told others about what I liked, they wouldn't believe it. She assured me of her secrecy, saying that she'd stay quiet because she loved my gifts. I took that conversation as a threat of blackmail. There was evidence in the way of photos on her phone and recordings.

I took the bait or, more accurately, I let her think I had.

In the last six months, Scarlett Barrack had kept her end of the bargain.

She hadn't told another soul.

She couldn't.

The locks on the doors and lack of communication with the outside world helped facilitate that silence. After all, since that conversation, she hadn't had a chance to speak to anyone—anyone besides Richard and me.

My chest inflated as I took another deep breath and turned the handle. Pushing the door to the suite inward, I found my answer to this long evening.

"Henri," Scarlett said as she stood in the doorway to the bathroom.

Her blond hair was piled on her head, and as I scanned her frame, I wondered what she was wearing beneath the white robe. It wouldn't matter. I'd have her exactly as I wanted her soon enough.

I locked the door behind me and turned back. My gaze narrowed and my voice dropped an octave. "Drop the robe, Scarlett."

She reached for the sash as she came closer. "I've missed you."

CHAPTER

8

Rae

My movement stalled as the steep trail ended on the soft, sandy beach. Catching my breath, I stood, mesmerized by the beauty. In many ways, it reminded me of my first date with Frankie. The dark, star-studded sky seemed to go on forever. As voices grew louder and more jovial, the moon glistened over the ocean and beach. The rhythm of waves crashing on nearby rocks and the steep incline all worked together to make this spot seem even more isolated.

Huge pieces of driftwood were arranged in a circle. I turned in time to watch as Chad and another guy pulled a large cooler from a small opening in the rocks.

"Drinks on the club," Beth said with a grin.

"How did they get here?"

She shook her head as she kicked off her sandals.

"Pete has a boat he keeps docked near the club. Throughout the day, a few beers make their way over to his boat. By sundown, the cooler is full. Before the dinner rush, he or someone else transports the cooler to this beach."

"So, you're stealing from the club?"

Beth grinned. "We like to think of it as reappropriating resources and aiding the club in its inability to provide sufficient employee benefits."

Chad lifted a bottle toward me. "Goldilocks, do you drink?"

"I mean, some..." I said as I also kicked off my sandals and made my way to him. Twisting the top, he handed me the bottle. The glass was cool in my grasp. Reading the label, I grinned. "No lime?"

"Remember, we're the help." Chad gestured about the beach. "Let me show you around."

When I turned to Beth, she was talking with Pete and another guy. "Sure," I said with an uncertain grin. "Is there that much to see?"

"More than you know."

My toes were covered in sand as we neared the waterline. Before reaching the ocean, Chad turned onto a small path I wouldn't have noticed if he weren't leading. Soon, we were climbing large rocks.

"Be careful of the tide pools," he said. "Some of the creatures can be sharp."

"Creatures?" I asked, stopping in place, recalling

the ones I'd seen with Frankie, the sea anemones he said could sting.

Chad lifted his free hand toward me, palm up. "Starfish, Goldilocks, not sharks."

Careful of where I stepped, I declined Chad's hand and stayed a step behind. In no time, we were high on a cliff. Overspray from the crashing waves below sprinkled our faces. A few steps back and the rocks were smooth and dry.

"Did Beth warn you about me?" Chad asked as we sat.

Tucking my dress around my knees, I nodded. "I was told to watch myself, or I'd end up a notch on your bedpost."

"Is that still a thing?"

"I don't know. It's a saying I remember my mom using."

Chad took a drink of his beer. "Where are you from?"

"Are you saying I don't seem like I was born and raised in Monterey?"

"If you were, I think I would have noticed you before now."

"Ohio, near Lake Erie. I moved out here three years ago." I grinned. "And I somehow stayed under your radar until today."

"That's not true. I noticed you when you came for the interview. Just so you know, I have ten bucks riding on you making it a week."

"Making it?" I asked.

"Staying on staff."

"A whole week. Wow, I'm overwhelmed by your confidence."

"Putting up with the asshole members gets old fast. McKenzie doesn't think you have what it takes."

The members like Frankie, or some of the gawking older men in the dining room?

"Did Beth bet?" I asked, wondering if my friend knew about this wager.

"She didn't, but she knows about it. We bet on every newbie." He leaned closer. "For the record, Beth thinks you'll make it. She's a nice girl, and I don't think she'd have recommended you if she didn't think you could cut it."

Sighing, I stared out at the dark water as the breeze blew my hair away from my face. "So far..." I wasn't sure if I trusted Chad, but then again, he made it easy to talk. "...it's not the members. I hardly noticed them. It's Mr. Kluser and..." I hesitated.

"McKenzie?"

"I hate being the new person anywhere."

"Says the girl who moved across the country."

"That was different," I said. "My dad died."

"I'm sorry."

"Me too. He was great. He's the one who called me Goldilocks. It was cancer. I don't like to think about it. He got sick right before my senior year of high school and went too quick. The good news was that it helped me qualify for some grants and scholarships. Near the end of my senior year, my mom remarried. Eric is nice enough, but he's younger than Mom, and for my graduation, I learned I was going to be a big sister."

"Whoa."

"Yeah, don't get me wrong. I'm happy for them." I shrugged. "I guess Mom's new life pushed me over the edge—the straw, so to speak. It wasn't hard to decide that it was time to move on." I looked out at the water. "Mom moved on with Eric and now Jendy, she's two. As much as I don't like being the newbie, I'm not a fan of being the reminder of the old—you know, that dress in the closet that doesn't fit anymore but you don't want to get rid of it?"

"The dress analogy is a little lost on me, but I get it."

I continued my answer. "My aunt and uncle live near San Francisco. She helped me find housing, and I know they're there if I need them. I guess I saw the opportunity and took it."

"I'm going to assume your dad didn't leave you a huge trust fund."

"That should be obvious by my current employment." I wiggled my sore toes. "Why do they want us to wear those shoes? My feet are killing me."

"I've heard it gets better." Chad nodded toward the beer. "Drink up and let it take the edge off."

"How about you? Are you from here?"

Chad drained the rest of the beer from his bottle

and laid it on the rock between us. "SoCal. Right now, I'm living the dream and working toward that surfer-dude goal."

"So kissing up to rich widows is the way to do that?"

"In all seriousness, I'm taking classes, trying to beef up my application for a doctorate in physical therapy."

"I'm seeing a theme—surfing and fitness."

Chad shrugged. "Mrs. Turner left me a five-hundred-dollar tip tonight."

My eyes opened wide. "Are you serious?"

He nodded. "We only have to share a percent. The tips add up. Mrs. Turner is a nice lady. She likes privacy and wants as little interaction between staff and her family as possible."

"How long have you worked here?"

"Going on three years."

"So, did you know the lady who died?"

He lifted his chin to the breeze and the surf. "Don't listen to gossip, Goldilocks."

"What do you think happened to her?"

"Money."

I placed my hands behind me and leaned back. "Five hundred dollars." I shook my head. "Maybe one day I'll get tips like that."

Chad's expression darkened. "Beth warned you against me. Let me warn you against some of the members. Never agree to work any off-site private parties, and watch how close you get to some of the men."

"Beth said that some members can be handsy."

"Not sure it's limited to the members." He paused. "No, I'm sure. It's not."

"What do you mean?"

"Do you know what money buys?" Chad asked in lieu of answering my question.

"Everything," I replied.

"Immunity."

Was he talking about the woman who died?

"From?" I asked.

"Everything. That immunity only works for the ones with the money. People like you and me..." He sighed. "Just watch yourself."

We both turned at the sound of laughter coming closer.

"Hey," Beth said, "no private parties."

"That's what I heard."

"Are you ready to go?" she asked.

I lifted my half-consumed beer. "I guess I could dump this."

Chad reached for the now-warmer bottle. "No fear. I'm here to save your beer." He grinned at Beth. "See, I'm a gentleman."

After we got back up to the top of the cliff, it wasn't until Beth and I were in her car that she asked what happened with Chad.

"He was right. He was a gentleman."

"No attempts to kiss you."

"Maybe I'm not his type. And I think I'm dating someone."

"Have you looked in a mirror? You're every man's type. Now, tell me about this maybe dating thing."

CHAPTER

9

Ashleigh Turner-Maxwell

Lifting back the blankets, I settled onto our bed as Caleb turned my way. My husband was propped up on two pillows with his tablet in his hand. "I'm worried about Henri."

Caleb exhaled and laid the tablet on his lap. "Well, don't. Your brother is a self-absorbed asshole who thinks the whole damn world owes him a living. I don't know why your mother puts up with his bullshit."

I squeezed the lotion bottle as a dollop squirted onto my palm. Rubbing my hands together, I laid my head back and looked up at the ceiling. I wasn't seeing the ornate woodwork or the textured surface. My thoughts were back at the country club. Mother had called us together to discuss the future of Turner Industries. We all knew the talk was coming. After our father died unexpectedly in a small plane crash off the coast, it was only a matter of time before she would tire of all the responsibility. That time had come.

As it was, my eldest brother Harry—Harrison to those not on his short list—had spent his entire life primed for succeeding our father.

He wasn't the only one.

I'd put in my time, too. Four years of undergrad at Stanford and an MBA from UCLA gave me the education my father thought was necessary. Although I was never given the responsibilities that our father gave to Harry, I had made my way up to the prestigious title of Vice President of Internal Relations. It was a fancy way to say that I oversaw our multiple locations, our regional managers, and our various expenses.

Harry might know more about the running of the mother ship, but when it came to making sure the satellites were operational and profitable, that was my doing. And the man at my side held an equally impressive title. His specialty was working with investors and keeping them happy. When Caleb and I married, I had been hesitant for him to enter the Turner Industries world. Maybe I'd been afraid he'd resent me or I'd end up resenting him.

That hadn't happened when my father was in control.

Over the last seven years since his death, Harry and our mother had worked together and kept Turner Industries profitable. In the current climate, that was an achievement.

"Do you think things will change once Mother hands the reins completely over to Harry?"

Caleb turned my way, his green eyes a bit cloudy. "Not for us."

"What does that mean?"

"Nothing."

I slipped my wedding rings back onto my freshly lotioned hands. "I know you and Harry are close. Am I right to be worried about Henri? He seemed...off tonight."

"Seriously, Ash. When doesn't your brother seem off?"

"He hasn't gotten over Ellen."

"Then he needs to grow the fuck up, confess, or move on. His aversion to the country club is ridiculous."

"Confess?" I refused to believe my brother had anything to do with what happened to Ellen. I remembered seeing him leave and Ellen still present at the Harvest Gathering. That's what I'd told the sheriff. I think it was what I recalled. I shook my head and thought of better things. "Ellen loved the country club." A grin came to my lips. "She, Marley, and I would have so much fun on the balcony. Sometimes even Mom would join us."

The balcony was a mostly—because they couldn't say all—women's location at the club. With a great view, pool, and bar, we could sip martinis and laugh for hours. "It hasn't been the same without her."

"I'm glad you can finally talk about her."

I shrugged.

"Ash, stop giving Henri that much power. You liked Ellen. You can remember her fondly. You decide your role with Harry and Turner Industries. If Henri wants to pout and make a spectacle out of himself, it's his right. Stop letting him pull you down."

"I introduced him to Ellen. I feel responsible."

"Were you the one who pushed her?"

"No. And we don't know that she was pushed."

"We don't know because your mother shut down the investigation."

"I don't like to see him" —my thoughts went back to dinner— "like he was tonight. Did you hear how rude he was to Chad?"

Caleb laid his tablet on the bedside stand and shook his head. "Your mother probably gave Chad a two-hundred-dollar tip. Do you think he really cares what Henri Turner says to him?"

"I don't know. I know Mom likes Chad. I would hope he doesn't refuse to be our server. She's so skeptical of anyone new."

"Two. Hundred. Dollar. Tip."

I scrunched my nose. "Do you think Chad thinks that's enough?"

Caleb grinned as he leaned my way. "Baby, some days I think you have the world figured out. And other times, I see you for who your parents raised you to be."

The lingering scent of Caleb's cologne tickled my

senses, and the warmth of his bare chest drew me nearer. "That's not true," I protested. "I understand the world better than my parents."

"Better than your mother?" He shook his head. "I'm not confident that's true. There are different worlds in that club. You wonder if two hundred dollars was enough. That's your world—our world. The other world sees two hundred and thinks that it's part of their rent or car payment or maybe it will buy groceries. For that world, two hundred is a fortune."

Sighing, I nodded. "You're right. I just know that Mom could leave a lot more. And with Henri being an ass, I think Chad deserved it."

Caleb's lips met mine as he pushed me back. His broad chest pressed against my breasts as his breaths deepened. I reached for his shoulders as his lips moved lower.

CHAPTER

10

Ashleigh

"Caleb." His name escaped my lips, maybe as a protest, but with the way my breathing had also deepened, I was unexpectedly aroused by his direct approach. Yet there was a part of me that felt the need to resist. "It's late. We both need to get up early."

His lips continued undeterred as he pushed one of my spaghetti straps over my shoulder and then the other. Lower his kisses went until they found my breasts. Each nipple was given his attention, licks and nips. The jolts shot through me from my breasts to my core.

My husband reached below the satin of my short nightgown, finding me bare beneath. His head popped up as his green eyes met mine. "Since when did you stop wearing panties to bed?"

I grinned as warmth increased beneath my skin. "It's not only to bed."

"Shit."

I scooted down and spread my knees as Caleb explored his new discovery, first with his fingers and then with his lips. It was easy to let myself be carried away by his ministrations. When we were first married —and before—our sex life was off the charts. We found excuses to be together. Whether it was turning down invitations from friends in the evening or even a quickie during our lunch hour, in the bathroom of a local deli, our sex life was exciting and new.

It was part of the reason I fell in love with Caleb. He never seemed interested in my name or my family's wealth and business. He was genuinely interested in me. Being with Caleb gave me a spark I found enticing and inviting. I was drawn to it like a moth to a flame. The way he made me feel was like something out of a love story novel or maybe an erotic romance. Just thinking about him could dampen my core and bring my nipples to attention.

That was fifteen years ago.

We vowed to never become "those" people— people who let life, work, and responsibility interfere with what mattered most. When we were twentysome-thing-year-olds, we were full of ideals. Probably like Chad or others who worked at the country club. Their possibilities weren't constricted by life's expectations. They were young and could view life as an open canvas—one waiting for the right muse or maybe the right color of chalk.

Six months ago, I'd asked Caleb for a divorce.

I didn't stop loving him.

I stopped liking him.

I stopped needing him.

It was a combination of coming to terms with Ellen's death and the questions her death raised. I kept wondering, if I died, had I really lived?

Caleb and I had done what we'd said we wouldn't: we drifted apart.

No, I didn't cheat.

What mattered more was that I didn't care if he had.

He moved out.

And then, after some time apart, we both realized we were willing to try. He was back home, and we'd been in counseling for the last four months.

Our divorce was on hold.

No one except us and my attorney even knew I'd asked for it. Caleb had stayed at our beach house, and no one was the wiser. My brothers would be livid. Harry would take my side, and I didn't want to end Caleb's career. It wasn't fair to him. I wasn't sure how my mother would have taken the news. I assumed she'd have been supportive to my face and then told Harry that I'd failed at the one thing a woman was supposed to do—be a wife.

Business hadn't been our mother's thing, not until

all three of us were older. She came into the fold in a less conventional way. There was no business school. My mother learned the secrets of being a shark in a boardroom from the best—my dad.

Since I'd decided to strip off my panties before coming to bed, I guess I could say that the counseling was working. And now as my nerves tingled in the aftermath of a mild tremor, I did my best to concentrate on the man above me.

My own essence combined with the taste of toothpaste as Caleb's and my tongues danced. His solid body pressed against mine as whispers of love and promises that were yet to be fulfilled filled my ears.

My back arched and my core stretched as we became one.

I let myself get lost in Caleb's rhythm, the sound of his breaths, and the warmth of his closeness. We fit together as we always had. He was both familiar and new. We were both open to exploring new ways to invigorate our sex life. Sharing those experiences with someone I'd loved for a large percentage of my life made them safe.

The counselor told me not to overthink. Yet as my body again ignited and small detonations went off, I couldn't help but overthink. I'd known my secret for two weeks, and I wanted to tell my husband.

It wasn't until we were once again two and I'd come back from cleaning myself that I settled next to Caleb and sighed.

"Stop worrying about Henri," he said, lifting his arm over my shoulder in the darkened bedroom and pulling me to his side.

For a moment, I took solace in the steady beat of his heart. "I'm not, at least not right now."

"Is it your mother?"

"No."

He turned my way. "All these years, Ash, I know there's something. What?"

Holding my breath, I confessed, "I'm pregnant."

CHAPTER

11

Rae

Closing my locker, I sighed. A week. I'd made it a week. Chad was partially right about the shoes. Either they'd gotten better or my feet were too numb to notice.

"Coming to the party?" Chad asked with a grin.

At the same time, I hit the button on the side of my phone, seeing two text messages from Frankie.

Looking at Chad, I grinned. "I'm seeing someone. I think."

"Well, there go my plans for ravishing you on the rock with the tide pools." He shook his head. "You're doing good, newbie. Come have fun."

Nodding, I said I would.

Next, I read the text messages.

"I miss you."

"Text me before I sound needy."

A grin curled my lips as I replied.

"I just got off work. I'm free tomorrow. Two whole days off."

Waiting, I stood with my back to the lockers as those around me shed their uniforms for more comfortable clothes.

"What's up?" Beth asked, looking at the phone in my hand.

I sighed. "I had missed texts from Frankie. I replied, but he's probably asleep by now."

"I never thought the Bowens would leave. It's almost midnight."

"Maybe I should head home."

"Come down to the beach for one beer or just to talk. Everyone is tired. It won't last long." She grinned. "After all, we need to clear the cooler so Pete has room for tomorrow's stash."

"I guess we all need to make sacrifices."

Soon I was wearing shorts and a sweatshirt, and Beth and I were walking the narrow path to the beach below. "Thanks," I said.

She turned, peering at me over her shoulder. "For what?"

"This job. The pay is good, and the tip share is better."

"You'll get to serve. When you do, the tips are even better."

Figures were coming to mind: rent, groceries, and utilities. My car was old and paid for. But that didn't mean I didn't have expenses there too—gas and maintenance.

When we reached the sandy shore, people were seated on the old driftwood with drinks in hand.

"Newbie," McKenzie said. "You made it."

I had.

A week.

"I did."

She lifted her beer. "Good job."

Soon, everyone was chatting, yet her simple compliment made me glad I'd decided to come down here. The more I got to know these people, the more I liked them.

Chad sat at my side and handed me an open beer. "So, who is this guy?"

I took the beer. "We met at Cal State."

"You like the brainy type."

I shrugged. "He's nice."

"You're saying that he hasn't tried to get in your pants?"

Sitting taller, I stared at Chad, who started to laugh after a few seconds. "Ease up, Goldilocks. If you like him, I'm sure he's a good guy."

I leaned toward Chad. "I like you too. Not in that way," I added quickly. My gaze went around the circle. "I like everyone here. I am surprised, but I do. I told you I hate being the new one, but everyone here made it bearable."

"But especially me." His smile glistened in the moonlight.

"Yeah, especially you."

"Thanks for not losing me money."

"I made it, but I'm going to sleep for the next two days."

"Good thing," he said. "Memorial Day weekend is coming."

"Is that big?"

"Bigger than big," Chad said.

Beth was right; the party didn't last long. We were all tired. Before long, we were all making our way back up to the cliffs.

My dark apartment welcomed me. Climbing into bed with my shorts and sweatshirt still on, I fell sound asleep. When I awoke, my stomach was growling, and the sun was streaming through my bedroom window. The clock on my phone said it was after one in the afternoon. It also signaled a text message.

"I think we're in two different time zones. How about dinner tonight?"

Staring up at the ceiling, I thought about the man who'd sent the text. Chad was right. Frankie was nice. He'd been a gentleman, holding hands, but nothing more. That didn't mean I hadn't thought about more.

Frankie was tall—taller than me—and when the sun hit his light-blue eyes, they sparkled like the sky over the ocean on a clear day. The grip of his hand was warm. I enjoyed his laugh and ease. Nothing seemed too much for him. Maybe that was because he came from the other side, the non-Muggles.

My smile dimmed as I worried about telling him where I worked.

What would he think?

Not everyone was born into wealth. That didn't make my family bad. My mom and Eric were hard workers, and my dad had been as well. I wasn't ashamed of what I was doing. I just didn't know how...

The words weren't coming.

I contemplated avoiding the impending conversation by telling Frankie I was busy.

Slipping from the bed, I went to the kitchen to start a pot of coffee and made a stop in the bathroom. My long light hair was a mess, and the makeup from last night left mascara smudges under my eyes. Stretching my arms, I grinned at my tussled reflection.

"You did it," I said to myself. "Chad won the bet, and McKenzie complimented me."

With a smile still on my lips, I went to my phone and texted Frankie.

"Not to sound needy, but I miss you too. What time and where?"

As I was drinking my coffee and reading emails, Frankie's response came through.

"Six o'clock. I could take you to the club."

While I wasn't sure when I'd confess my employment, I knew I wasn't ready. I replied.

"I have to wear heels at work. Do you mind something more casual?"

His reply dinged right away.

"As long as I get to be with you, I'm open for sandwiches in the park."

My coffee settled in my stomach as I nodded and replied.

"It's a date."

CHAPTER

12

Henri

I read the note from my assistant, Lucy, the one left on my desk when I entered the office. The first four subjects were normal doings, calls and emails to be returned. It wasn't even eight o'clock in the morning, and Lucy had three emails ready in my draft folder. If I okayed them, it was simply a matter of hitting send. The fourth line caused my jaw to clench.

Ashleigh wants to meet you for lunch.

A week had passed since our family meal at the country club. If I had my way, family time was not in need of replenishing anytime soon.

My sister was the self-proclaimed one in our family to oversee everything. Sometime over the last seven years, what our mother stopped doing, Ashleigh did. I couldn't blame Mother for being more self-absorbed as time passed. Hell, she had the money to do whatever her heart desired. The fact that she was still involved in Turner Industries meant one thing as far as I was concerned. It meant she didn't have faith in Harry's ability to handle the top spot alone.

In reality, I'd rather have Mother's attention on the dealings of Turner Industries than on the personal lives of her children and grandchildren. Harry and Marley's boys were both in high school this coming autumn. The eldest would be a junior, and Tim, the youngest, would be a freshman. Or maybe they achieved those levels at the end of the previous school year.

Keeping up on the activities of children interested me as much as lunch with my sister. Thankfully, procreation wasn't in my future. Fate had made one good decision.

"Mr. Turner," Lucy said as she opened my office door. "I have your coffee, and Lewis Dewalt is on line two."

"Thank you, Lucy. I need a whole pot for this conversation."

She stepped inside my office, carrying the mug of coffee to my desk.

I would be blind not to notice the way her blouse and skirt fit, showing me only a hint of the curves beneath, or the way the high heels made her shapely legs appear. At nearly ten years my junior, Lucy was one of the best assistants I'd had, and I was determined not to lose her to sexual harassment charges.

Nevertheless, as she turned my way, I couldn't stop the image of her falling to her knees and opening her painted lips, begging for my cock.

"Do you want me to transfer the call?" she asked.

Taking a deep breath, I pushed away my illicit thoughts of how talented she would be at sucking me off as I took a seat behind my desk, my cock suddenly hardening beneath my suit pants. I unbuttoned my suit coat, confident I'd sat before Lucy could notice my arousal. I lifted the coffee. "Yes, transfer the call, and then call my sister and tell her I have a lunch engagement. We can try for another day."

Lucy stopped midstep and turned my way. Her pretty painted lips were no longer smiling. "I'm sorry."

After taking a small drink of the coffee, I set the cup down and looked her way. "Sorry. Why?"

"Before mentioning lunch, Mrs. Maxwell asked about your schedule. She knows you don't have a lunch engagement. I told her."

"Fuck," I mumbled. "Fine. Tell her I'll meet her at the deli on Pine at noon. And call ahead for a table."

The Fresh Deli on Pine Street didn't take reservations, officially. There were definite perks in this city and beyond with the last name Turner.

"Yes, sir."

Seconds after Lucy closed the door, a light blinked on my phone, indicating the waiting call. Before answering, I adjusted my erection, a bit surprised after the workout I'd given it the last few nights—or should I say, Scarlett gave it—that I was so easily aroused. Her suite had been my distraction since the last episode with my family.

I took the call.

"Henri," Lewis Dewalt, the man in charge of my personal investments, spoke through the phone. "I was wondering how you would feel about a new venture."

My mind went to the woman in my home. Maybe I was getting bored with her being so complaisant. There was no arguing she could not only give a great blow job, but she was also much better at understanding her role and my unique desires. Nevertheless, a challenge would be inviting.

I could take Lucy, but that would mean finding a new assistant.

"Do I have your interest, Henri?"

I spun my chair toward the windows overlooking the ocean and leaned back, removing the pressure from my cock. "Yes, Lewis. New sounds intriguing. Tell me more."

There was nothing like a fifteen-minute discussion on the futures of cryptocurrency and the appreciation to investing in art to ease the ache of an erection. By the time I hung up, my circulation was back on target, and I forced my thoughts to go to the dealings of the day.

Lost down a rabbit hole of expenditures, I was surprised by a knock on the office door.

I looked at the clock on the corner of my computer screen. It was ten until twelve. "Come in."

Lucy opened the door and stepped in. "Sir, your sister."

"Fuck," I said, standing and reaching for the suit coat I'd taken off earlier. "Call her and tell her I'm running five minutes late."

"Do you want me to get you a car?"

"No. Hell, walking is quicker." It was, and from the view beyond my windows, it was a beautiful late spring day. As I stepped past Lucy, I added, "And call the deli. I'll take the chicken pecan salad and a tea. The sooner the food arrives, the sooner I can be done with my sister."

Lucy grinned. "Yes, sir."

CHAPTER

13

Ashleigh

The Fresh Deli wasn't far from the office building that housed the headquarters of Turner Industries. I half expected to see Henri when I went down the final staircase into the lobby. I considered waiting, texting, or calling. We could walk the few blocks together, and maybe I could set the tone, one where he might actually talk to me.

However, once it neared noon, I decided to walk alone.

Shelly, one of the deli's owners, came to me as soon as I entered, telling me that Henri's assistant had asked for a reserved table near the windows and had sent Henri's order ahead. After walking me to the table, she chatted for a moment before taking my order.

Beyond the tall windows, the sun shone on the lawn and outside patio. If Henri hadn't reserved this table, I would have suggested that today would be a great day for dining outside.

"Here's your lemonade," Shelly said with a smile. "If he stands you up, I'll hold the bill for him."

"Thanks, Shelly. If he stands me up, he'll owe me for more than a lunch."

"I'm glad Mr. Turner has you around."

"I'm not sure he is, but thanks."

I checked my emails on my phone and sipped my drink as I waited. A news bulletin came across my screen. Before reading it, I saw a familiar face. It wasn't Henri I saw but Chad, from Woodland. "Chad," I called.

Yes, I was married, working on that marriage, and newly pregnant, but I had eyes and they worked as I scanned Chad from his canvas loafers, up his toned legs, khaki shorts, and dry-fit shirt. It wasn't like he was a kid. Chad was easily in his mid-twenties.

Men could look at younger women; why couldn't women look at younger men?

My attention went to the bulge in the front of his shorts. No doubt, there was something lost under the black pants and white shirt he wore at the club. The prominent protrusions and tight angles were on full display in his current attire. Chad's gaze came my way seconds before a smile came to his lips.

"Mrs. Maxwell."

I reached for my purse and opened my wallet. "I'd

like to thank you for being so nice to my mother. I know that not everyone in my family is as friendly."

Chad waved away my gesture. "No need, Mrs. Maxwell. Mrs. Turner is more than generous, and I appreciate her always asking for me."

Folding a hundred-dollar bill, I handed it his direction. "Please, this is from my husband and me. Your hard work doesn't go unnoticed, and sometimes my mother is less giving than she should be."

He shook his head. "I can't take that, but thank you." He nodded. "Have a good day."

"You too, Chad," I replied, a bit surprised he wouldn't take the cash.

I tucked the bill back in my billfold and, after securing it in my purse, placed the strap over my chair. When I turned, I was met by my brother's grin.

"You didn't give that leech more money, did you?"

I sat taller. "Hi, Henri. It's great to see you again. I'm sorry I didn't say goodbye the other night, but you left rather abruptly."

Unbuttoning his suit coat, Henri let out a breath and sat in the chair across the table from me. "Dinner was over. I enjoy small talk with our family about as much as others enjoy waterboarding."

"It's not that bad."

"Worse, if you ask me." He looked around. "I thought my salad would be here by now."

"Take another breath. I told them to wait until you arrived to bring it out."

Henri looked at his watch. "I have a call in—"

"Two hours, according to Lucy. I won't keep you that long."

Henri's jaw clenched as he sat straighter. "If this is your biweekly check-in, I'm fine."

"Are you?"

"What the fuck does that mean?"

"Shh," I scolded, leaning forward. "Take it down a notch. You're constantly on edge."

My brother leaned back as a strange glint came to his eyes. "I'm fine, Ash. I just prefer spending my evenings without the blessing of family. Besides, I'm working to keep my options open. Once Harry pushes Mom out of Turner Industries, I'll be unemployed."

"You won't, but so what? You could live your life at sea, if you wanted, on a fancy big boat."

"So could you and Caleb." He paused as Shelly delivered our salads. Once she was gone, he continued, "Or is this visit to tell me that you're finally divorcing his ass and sailing on a solo journey."

"No, Caleb and I are good."

"Right." Henri reached for his fork. "And Harry is going to give me the keys to the kingdom once he has the power."

"I just wanted to be sure you were all right."

"I am, Ash. No need to worry. I don't plan to make a public spectacle of myself again anytime soon. I just don't care for the club. I don't know why Mother insists on eating there. Hell, order pizzas and eat at her place."

"Maybe she wants an excuse to go out. She feels comfortable there."

He wiped his lips with the napkin. "I don't like it—especially the dining room. The help there look at Mother as if she's made of money. That Chad is the worst of the bunch."

"By doing what, waiting the table?" I tilted my head toward the lunch counter, where Shelly was talking to another customer. "Is Shelly guilty too? Maybe we need to keep an eye on all servers. It could be a conspiracy. I think they refill our coffee just to get an extra dollar." Sarcasm dripped from my words.

"Don't say I didn't warn you."

"Warn me about what?" I asked.

"Chad. He seems like he's up to something. You never know what goes on in the head of a person like that."

"A person like *that*? Like what?" When he didn't respond, I confessed to my earlier attempt to give him money. "I offered Chad an extra tip for last night."

Henri's forehead furrowed. "Why?"

I didn't want to tell him it was because I thought he, Henri, had been an ass. "I think exceptional service should be rewarded."

"Well, you've done your good deed for today. Did you get a receipt? The accountants can turn it into a write-off—donations to the poor."

As Shelly took away our plates, my phone buzzed.

It was the news bulletin I'd ignored earlier. The

picture on the screen was of a pretty blond young lady. I paused as I looked at her picture.

"What is it?" Henri asked.

I lifted my phone to show him the screen. "This woman. She looks familiar. Do you recognize her?"

Henri sat straighter. "No."

I began to read. "It says here that after being missing since last autumn, the Woodland Sheriff's Department is launching an investigation. Apparently, her cousin has made numerous calls and hasn't been able to reach her, not hearing from her in months." I continued to read. "Oh, she worked at the Cliffs Country Club. Law enforcement now believes there may be more to her disappearance." I looked up to my brother's blank expression. "Are you sure you don't remember her?"

Henri pulled two twenties from his money clip and laid them on the table. "I do have a call, Ash, one I forgot to tell Lucy about." He forced a smile. "Thanks for checking on me. I'll make an effort to grace the Cliffs with my presence." He straightened his shoulders. "Really, I'm good. Glad you and Caleb are too." He stood. "I need to go. Give Shelly whatever is left and keep her off my list of leeches."

Henri didn't wait for me to reply before he walked away.

CHAPTER

14

Rae

E veryone around the country club was in high gear. Memorial Day was approaching, and according to all of the kitchen and dining room staff, this coming weekend was one of the biggest and busiest times of the year. Superwealthy members came from all around—the state, country, and even the world—to attend the three-day extravaganza.

Carrying a load of plates to the conveyor belt, I noticed the way Mr. Kluser was staring down at his phone. Usually, he was looking over his domain like a lion. No, it was more like a serpent, narrowing his eyes. Maybe a rattlesnake, ready to strike.

"Watson, pick up the pace," he called over the din of the kitchen.

Turning on my heel, I headed back to the floor. We had three tables of members recently leave and three families waiting to enter. Just before I reached the swinging door, Mr. Kluser grabbed my upper arm and pulled me toward him. His abrupt change in my direction had me wobbling on my tall heels. I steadied myself as I looked up at his expression, my pulse suddenly thumping wildly.

"You're not the newbie anymore. Get your shit together."

I sucked in a breath, my nostrils flaring while I worked to keep my rebuttal buried.

"Ten minutes," he said. "Get the tables turned and come back to my office."

My eyes opened wide. "I don't know what you want. I'm moving as fast as everyone else."

"My office." He released my arm.

Quickly, I hurried back to the dining room, not fully certain if I was pissed off, nervous, upset, or all three. My emotions were scattered as it was. I hadn't seen Frankie in nearly a week. He texted but claimed he was too busy to get away.

I couldn't help but wonder if his reasoning was true or if he had seen me here at the club. I didn't want to broach the subject over text messages.

On top of that, my mom, her husband, and my sister wanted to visit. Eric had the unusual opportunity for time off during the holiday, but I knew that with all the preparations, I would be lucky to have a few hours off in the mornings. As I was trying to get them to reconsider the timing of their visit, my mother used Jendy as blackmail. "But, Rae, your sister wants to see you. She wants you to show her the beach."

Lately, the only beach I'd been to was the off-limits beach on the club's property.

I was starting to believe that I returned to the after-work party each night because I liked the camaraderie. Being there gave me a sense of belonging, more than any other reason. On the beach was the only time that everyone on staff could relax and talk. During those conversations, I was also learning some interesting bits of information—or was it gossip—about many of the members and their families. So far, no one had mentioned the Hamiltons—Frankie's family.

Maybe that meant they weren't the troublemakers that some of the other members could be.

After clearing the third table before Pete set it for the next members, I deposited the last utensils and glasses in the kitchen and looked around. Mr. Kluser wasn't at any of his normal posts, watching everything that was happening. A quick glance confirmed that his office door was closed.

Taking a breath, I began walking toward Mr. Kluser's office. I'd been in there the day I was hired, filling out tax forms and signing my name to many pages of rules, including a nondisclosure statement.

If talking to the other servers was part of that agreement, I didn't know anyone on staff who hadn't broken it. Thankfully, where we congregated nightly on the property was safe from security or surveillance.

My skin prickled with anticipation as I straightened my black skirt and entered the small hallway, toward Mr. Kluser's office door.

Beth stepped from the staff ladies' room, blocking my path only a few yards from his door. Her green eyes narrowed in question. "Where are you going?"

"Mr. Kluser told me to go to his office."

Beth inhaled and stood taller, as tall as her petite frame would allow. "Don't go."

I shook my head. "Beth, I can't lose this job. When I was hired, I quit my other one. Already with tips, I've made more than I would have in twice the time at the store."

She reached for my hand and turned me toward the kitchen. "We have three new tables, and there are reservations until after ten. Keep working. Don't stop. If Max says something, tell him you were so carried away with work that you forgot."

My stomach twisted. "What's going on?"

"You've been here a few weeks, right?"

I nodded.

"Three?"

"Yeah. Why is that important?"

"We lose more people in the first week than after, except for the third week."

The first week made sense. Woodland Cliffs was a different world, even from working in regular restaurants. "Why the third week?" I asked with more dread than I anticipated.

"Let's go have a drink after work."

"On the beach with the others?"

Beth shook her head. "No. Alone. I should have been more open. I'm sorry."

She pulled me toward the swinging door. I turned back one more time, looking at the closed office door.

"Are you sure I won't get in trouble?"

"No," Beth answered. "But as my friend, not just someone I met here, I want you to know the trouble that's waiting on the other side of that door."

My eyes widened.

A man I didn't recognize came through the swinging door. Although I didn't know him, something about his appearance, not only his expensive suit, but his demeanor, said he was important. He stopped, coming face-to-face with Beth and me. His gaze lingered a bit on Beth before turning to me. "Where is Mr. Kluser?"

"He's in his office," I replied.

"What's your name?" he asked.

"Rae, Rae Watson."

"They need help in the Tertian Lounge. You're reassigned for the rest of the night."

Beth's expression hardened as her jaw clenched.

Without another word, the man headed toward Kluser's closed door.

"Why didn't he have you go up there?" I asked Beth. "You've been here longer."

She shook her head. "Find me when you're done. We need to talk."

"What's going on?"

The man entered Mr. Kluser's office without a knock.

"That was Bernie Maze. There are a few families, such as the Turners, who have the bulk of the stock in the club. However, it's the board of executives who make the decisions. When it comes to that board" — she tilted her chin— "he's one of the top. CFO." Beth smiled. "And if I'm right about something else, Max was just caught with his pants down."

"Because he wasn't on the floor?"

"No, Goldilocks. Literally."

CHAPTER

15

Henri

Ignoring the other members, I made my way to the bar in the Cliffs' gentlemen's suite and took a barstool near the end of the shiny bar. As much as I detested this club, I appreciated the gentleman's suite, especially without my family present. The rich red leather of the chair was lost on me as I studied the bottles lining the shelf in front of the large mirror. My choice of a seat to the side kept me from looking directly into the reflection.

I wasn't sure whose idea it was to put mirrors behind bars, but I found the practice exhausting. Was it because the tried-and-true drinkers found their soul mate in that reflection? Or could it be that it gave those sitting on the stools a view of the world behind them?

Maybe it started in the Wild West. A cowboy had to watch for enemies as he downed his whiskey.

The mirror over this bar would only show me clusters of chairs, plush high-backed chairs and soft barrel chairs arranged in circles for the enjoyment of groups of people. I wasn't a group. I was singular, and at this moment, I didn't need to be reminded.

"Mr. Turner, what can I get you?" Bette, the buxom bleached blonde, asked.

"What are my options, Bette?"

Her painted lips curled. "I never could turn you down, Henri." She tilted her chin. "Maze is here right now, entertaining some out-of-state members. I can't step away until later."

Hell, I wasn't sure I wanted what she was offering, but then again, I might be sure later. It was best to keep my options open. "I'll take Black Label. Leave the bottle right here." I patted the bar. "I promise, I'm good for it."

"Oh," she said with a grin. "I know that."

A few minutes later, I had a tumbler in my hand with two fingers of Black Label and a bottle ready to keep pouring.

"I didn't expect to see you here," my brother Harry said as he took the stool to my side.

"Fuck, Harry, go away."

"It's always good to see you too, brother." He lowered his voice. "Seriously, what are you doing here? Reminiscing? Is this the anniversary? Not a year, six months?"

"Fuck you," I said as I lifted the tumbler to my lips and swallowed the entire contents of the glass.

"Don't sit here alone, Henri." Harry lifted his chin toward one cluster of chairs. "Caleb is here too. Have you heard the news?"

I turned toward the chairs, taking in the smug, smiling faces, and then turned back. "From their expressions, he's celebrating. Is he finally leaving Ashleigh, or did she get word of his philandering ways and kick his ass to the curb?"

"Get your head out of your ass."

I smirked as I poured another drink.

"Ashleigh is pregnant."

I spun toward him. "Well, good for our sister. Who's the lucky father?"

"You know, Henri, Caleb would want to crack you across the jaw for that. And if he did, I wouldn't lift a finger to help you."

"Of course not. You never have."

"Bullshit," he growled near my ear. "July 1st, Turner Industries transfers to me. Get your ass up and congratulate our brother-in-law, or July 2nd, I'm throwing you out of the building." He barely paused. "But don't worry, Ellen's case will remain closed until Mother passes. Good news, there's no statute of limitations on murder."

"I left the club, Harry. I wasn't here."

"You two fought."

"You're right," I said. "Why the fuck do you think I'm beating myself up six months later? I'm guilty of leaving Ellen here, nothing else." I lifted my glass and stood, straightening my shoulders. "I'll congratulate Caleb and then excuse myself. Let me go, Harry. And as for July 2nd, we'll see."

My elder brother shook his head.

As I stood, he walked beside me. And always the politician, he patted my shoulder as he announced to the group of men, "Look who I found."

"Henri," was said by all—all except Caleb.

I feigned a smile. "I hear congratulations are in order. I didn't hear the news until now, but" —I lifted my glass— "congratulations. To my future niece or nephew."

Caleb lifted his glass along with the others and took a sip. "Thank you, Henri."

"Now, if you'll excuse me."

I turned toward my stool as a waitress I didn't recognize walked up to the bar. My feet stilled as she leaned forward, talking to Bette, her cute, tight ass pushed back. I scanned lower to her shapely legs and high black heels.

Ellen used to say that the women here wore "fuck me" heels as an advertisement. If that was the case with this new beauty, I was an interested buyer. First, I'd need to test-drive the merchandise.

For only a moment, I had a thought about the woman I'd asked to marry me, the one I lost half a year ago. She wouldn't approve of where my attention had gone; then again, she wouldn't approve of my fuck toy back at the mansion either.

It seemed I was a disappointment on every level.

Retaking my seat at the bar, I saw Harry's smiling face out of my peripheral vision.

A disappointment who was about to be unemployed.

"Mr. Turner," Bernie Maze said, walking up next to me at the bar. "You wanted to speak to me about something?"

Fuck. I did.

I lowered my voice. "Have there been any concerns regarding that server Chad?"

"In the dining room?"

"Yes." I shook my head. "I'm concerned that he has motives."

"Motives, Henri, what are you saying? Did you observe something?"

"I'm not comfortable with how he interacts with my mother. It's too friendly."

Bernie's eyes narrowed. "Of course, you're against friendly behavior."

"When it comes to my mother, yes. And the other night when she got home, she couldn't find her bracelet. She's certain she wore it. I think it was stolen."

"From her wrist?"

"Frail old thing. She wouldn't even notice if someone pulled it off."

"I'll look into this. I promise."

"Thank you, Bernie."

My mother was neither frail nor without a bracelet. It was the best story I could come up with on short notice. I was as ready for her to leave Turner Industries as she was. Truth be told, I stayed involved in the family company for her. Lately, I'd been acquiring an interest in multiple investments. Along with crypto and art, I was working on a possible partnership with a vineyard business. Mitchell Hamilton and I were onto something, a deal that would make both of us wealthy —wealthier beyond our wildest dreams. I didn't care what Harry did with Turner Industries once he was in charge. I'd wipe that shit from my shoes and move on. He wouldn't need to wait until July 2nd. I'd have my letter of resignation on his desk first thing the morning of the first.

I reached out as the pretty blonde came past.

"Oh, excuse me," she said, stepping away from my touch.

"What's your name, pretty girl?"

A flush of pink filled her cheeks in the most provocative of ways.

"Rae. My name's Rae."

"Why haven't I seen you before?"

She shifted a bit. "Tonight's my first night in the Tertian Lounge."

That was the real name given to this gentlemen's lounge, back when the club was founded.

I pulled my money clip from the pocket of my pants and stripped off a C-note. "Here, sweetheart, I'm going to go to that empty table. Make sure no one bothers me and my bottle doesn't empty." I grinned. "And I'll double that at the end of the night."

She hesitated for a second or more.

It was fucking adorable.

My cock twinged.

Maybe this was exactly what I needed, someone new in my life, someone to take my mind off the mundane day-to-day torture of life's ups and downs. Yeah, this little lady might be wet behind the ears, but if I had my way, she'd also be wet between her legs.

As I settled at the corner table with my tumbler, Rae followed with a full bottle of Black Label. She placed it in the center of the table. "Here you go, Mr. Turner. Let me know if you need anything else."

With my cock hardening, I replied, "I definitely will."

CHAPTER

16

Rae

Wearing only soft shorts and a tank top, I dried my hair with a towel and made my way out into the living room of my apartment. On the couch with a nearly empty bottle of rosé was Beth.

"I'm sorry," I said, tossing the towel through the bathroom door to the sink as I ran my fingers through my hair. "I felt gross."

"Yeah, Henri Turner can do that to a person." She looked up at me with her green eyes. "How much did he tip you?"

"A hundred at first and then a second hundred. After sharing, he alone tipped more than I would make in a day at the store." I shrugged. "He said there was more..." I let my words trail away as I pushed away the innuendos of his offer. Curling my legs beneath me, I plopped down at the other end of the sofa and, leaning forward, poured the remainder of the wine in my glass. When I sat up, Beth was looking at me. "I told him I was busy." I forced a smile. "Hanging out with a friend."

"Did he ask you if you have a boyfriend?"

I rolled my eyes. "After he thoroughly checked out my left hand."

She shook her head. "That wasn't all he was checking out."

I shivered. It wasn't the temperature of the apartment as much as the memories. "I'm not for sale." After taking a drink, I leaned back. "Now, what do you want to tell me?"

She shrugged. "You are, Rae. I'm sorry, but that's what working at the Cliffs is. It's a constant give-and-take. Mostly, they want to take."

"I am what? What do you mean?"

For a moment, my friend chewed her lip. Then she finished the wine in her glass, scooted over toward the coffee table, and, using the corkscrew, began opening the second bottle. With a new full glass, Beth sighed and leaned back against the couch. "Remember what Chad said, about bets?"

"Yeah, I get it. I've placed a few on recent new hires."

"I knew you had what it took to make it here—there. And damn, the money can be good. I've watched you struggling—financially. After your roommate moved out, I know you almost lost this place."

"Now I have the bedroom all to myself. Gone are the twin beds."

"I hoped the Cliffs would help."

"And I appreciate it. I really do. Hell, tonight's tips alone will help. If I can get placed in the lounge a few more times, I could actually have a savings account."

Beth looked down in her glass as she twisted the stem and the liquid swirled. When she looked back up, her eyes were cloudy. "What are you willing to do for that savings account?"

"Nothing happened tonight. I can put up with some handsy assholes for a few hours."

"But what if something was expected to happen?"

"Is this about Mr. Kluser, what you were saying about his pants being down?"

Beth nodded. "Three weeks is usually his time. By then, the girl has proven she can handle the work, and she's gotten a taste of the money. Not the salary, though it's not terrible, but the tips. By then, he thinks he's got you."

Though I knew the answer, I wanted to hear it. "Why did he want me in his office?"

"Most likely a blow job."

As I closed my eyes, my chest felt heavy. "Eww."

Beth grinned. "Don't tell me you're an oral virgin."

"I'm not." I wasn't. "But it's been with guys I know, like, or think I like. Sometimes I'm a bad judge of what's good and what's not." Another thought popped into my tired mind. "Have you? With him?"

"Every female who's been in the kitchen or dining room for over three weeks has."

"McKenzie? June? Gloria?"

With each name, Beth nodded. "If you want to stay employed, you will too. I guess I didn't want you blind-sided like I was."

I shook my head. "No. Tell someone. Tell that bigwig guy, Maze. If we go to the board united, they'll have to listen to us."

"Sleeping with Maze got you your job."

"No." I stood, placing the wineglass on the table. "I'm not sleeping with him. I saw him in the lounge tonight. He has a wedding ring."

"Not you, me. And yeah, Max is married too. They don't care."

Sighing, I sat back on the couch. "Damn, I need to quit."

"Really? Are you so high and mighty that you'll be homeless over blowing a guy? From experience and stories, it's less than five minutes of degradation." She smiled. "Personally, I think it was closer to two. Touch his balls, and you might make him come even quicker. He isn't known for his endurance. From stories, he didn't even last one minute with Scarlett."

"Stories?"

"Yeah, hers," Beth said, her smile growing as she shook her head. "Scarlett was something else. Do you want to know her secret?"

I shook my head as I scrunched my nose. "I don't think I do."

"She'd lick her finger, and once he was in her mouth, she'd tease his asshole."

"No. I did not want to know that."

Ugh. I'd taken a shower, but now I needed a brain clean. The images in my mind were ones I hoped would be gone in the morning. Reaching again for my wineglass, I hurriedly drank the contents before refilling the entire globe. I turned to Beth. "I'm not high and mighty, but this isn't right. If we all—"

"If we *all*," she interrupted, "stand up together, we'll *all* get fired. Every one of us can be replaced. They know that. We do too."

"Then we go to the media. I don't know, social media, the local news."

"We signed an NDA."

Beth's confession had me connecting dots. "So it's not just once?"

"No."

I can't do this.

"Wait," I said as I remembered what she'd just told me, "you slept with that guy? Maze?"

Beth nodded.

"Oh Beth, you didn't have to do that to get me a job."

"I didn't. I did it to keep my job, but I thought I could try for more." She shrugged. "It worked. You're hired."

"Why didn't he pick you to go to the gentlemen's lounge tonight?"

"I guess in his mind, it's my turn."

"Your turn?" I asked.

"Another night in a hotel or maybe simply a blow job in his office and I'll get the assignments again. I think that choosing you with me standing there was meant as a reminder that he makes the decisions."

"God, I've never felt this way."

"What way?"

"Like I'm trapped."

"Or," Beth said, "you can think about it another way. Don't give them the power. Use the power. Scarlett taught me that. Make them want you and then use it." She shrugged. "If Bernie had given me the assignment, it could mean he didn't want me again. What he did was his way of saying he does."

Sighing, I set my glass on the table. "This—all of this—goes against everything I believe."

"I understand. I have a couch if you need a place to live for a while."

Crossing my arms over my chest, I leaned back against my own couch. "Shit, this sucks."

"Not tonight, but it will."

CHAPTER

17

Ashleigh

"What did you tell them, dear?" Mother asked as she took a seat on the love seat on the balcony of Caleb's and my home.

"It wasn't that big of a deal. They came to the office." I shrugged. "I don't know a thing. Apparently, her name is Scarlett Barrack, and she used to work at the country club."

My mother shook her head as her soft gray eyes stayed laser focused on me. "As significant investors in the Cliffs, we need to watch every word we say."

I shook my head and shrugged. "I didn't say anything. I don't know anything. I really don't remember her."

Mother's lips pursed as she sat taller. "Very well. In the future, I think it would be better if you simply referred all questions to Lloyd."

"Lloyd handles our personal legal business. This wasn't personal."

"Lloyd oversees the firm with all our representation. Yes, we keep different entities under different shingles for tax purposes and to avoid the appearance of impropriety, but if the police contact you again, call Lloyd and he'll know what to do."

I inhaled, taking in the fresh sea breeze as I watched the sunlight dance on the ocean's waves. Without thinking, I laid my hand over my midsection.

"How are you feeling?" my mother asked.

"All right. I'm most nauseated when I first wake. As long as I keep nibbling, I'm better as the day progresses."

"Nibbling—aren't you concerned about weight gain?" Mother shook her head. "You'll be forty when this baby is born. Do you really think that's wise?"

My gaze narrowed. "Excuse me?"

"I'm worried about you. If you and Caleb need a child to fix your marriage, maybe it shouldn't be fixed."

I couldn't believe my ears.

Standing, I went to the railing and lifted my face to the sun, taking in its strength and warmth, before turning back to my mother. "Caleb's and my marriage is fine. We're both very excited about starting a family. This isn't forty years ago when you were pregnant with me. My doctor is watching everything."

"Sometimes, it's better not to take a risk."

"You're talking about your grandchild."

"As I said, my concern is you, Ashleigh. I was hoping you would be a bigger help to Harrison once we made the succession final. How can you be helpful when you're suffering from morning sickness or caring for a child? I do hope you have some friends who know of a good nanny or, better yet, maybe an au pair." She nodded. "Yes, we looked into an au pair when Henri was born."

My mind filled with too many comebacks, things I wanted to say about priorities and the fact that the child inside me was Caleb's and mine, not my mother's. Decisions were ours. Instead, I tilted my head and plastered on my best smile. "Oh, no need to worry, Mother. You see, my due date isn't until December. By then, you'll be fully retired from the company. Caleb and I wanted to propose a question."

She sat taller. "What question?"

"Since you'll have free time, we thought perhaps you'd like to move in with us and be a full-time grandmother."

It took all my self-control not to break out in a fit of laughter as my mother's expression morphed from shock to fear and finally to amusement.

"You know," she said, "I would love to spend time with not only your baby but Harry's boys. However, instead of making a commitment to that, I suggest you create a list of names of reputable nannies and a good au pair service. Make sure they're bonded. Oh, have Lloyd do a background check. And of course, whomever you hire will need to sign an NDA."

"You're simply full of legal advice today."

"Oh, well, yes. No more detectives, Ashleigh. Not without representation."

"I still don't know what your concern could be. The girl is an adult. She's been gone for nearly six months. Maybe she met someone and was whisked to a tropical paradise, or maybe she OD'd and is gone forever. The Cliffs can't be held responsible for every employee."

Mother took a deep breath, looked down at her lap, and then back to the sparkling ocean. "I'd rather Henri not be questioned."

My stomach twisted as I went back to the wicker chair and sat, gripping the arms. "Why would that be a problem?"

She straightened her neck and shoulders before she turned to me. "The girl disappeared not long after Ellen's unfortunate accident. Your brother is coping the best he can."

My thoughts went back over the past six months. "He's coping."

"Yes, but I'm concerned about the future."

"How does that woman's disappearance fit into those concerns?"

Mother stood. "It doesn't," she said definitively,

moving her lips to a straight line. "Just do our family a favor, Ashleigh, and no more speaking to the authorities without representation. I've also spoken my wishes to your brother, but I'm tired. Stepping down from Turner Industries is meant to be just that—stepping down, not into legal problems, family legal problems."

My brother.

Which one?

"Do you mean Harry?" I asked.

"I'll need to respect his wishes and believe that any of his decisions, no matter if I agree, are in the best interest of Turner Industries and your father's dream."

My mother was good at doing that, mentioning our father when she wanted to get her way.

"That is why," she continued, "I hope Harry will be able to count on you. Especially if Henri is no longer involved, it's not a good time for you to be distracted."

Again, I laid my hand over my midsection.

I wasn't showing. My clothes all still fit. There were no flutters or movements such as the ones in the book about expecting. Nevertheless, I felt a connection to the tiny person within me and a fierce need to protect him or her.

"I'm sure everything will work out," I said as I met her standing.

"Always the optimist." Mother turned toward the opening, peering into our home before looking back.

"Ashleigh, it isn't that I'm not thrilled with the prospect of your child. You're my daughter, and it's right that I should worry. I also know, from experience, that it's too easy for women to be defined by their family." She reached out and took my hand. "You have already defined yourself as a competent, strong business-woman. You know that I'm proud of what you've accomplished, as was your father. It pains me to think that you will throw that away."

"I'm not throwing anything away. Unless Harry's plans for me are similar to his for Henri, I'll find a way to manage both, a career and a family."

She nodded. "That's what I needed to hear from you."

I was pretty sure she could have gone about that fishing trip in a better way. "May I see you out?"

We walked in silence through the great room and down the hallway to the foyer. After my obligatory kiss on her cheek, my mother stepped through the front door, her car and driver waiting in my driveway. Once the door was closed, I exhaled and leaned against the hard wooden barrier, my phone in my pocket vibrating.

"They say you learn a lot about parenting from your parents." I splayed my fingers over my stomach. "Don't worry, little one. Your mommy can learn what not to do, too. Your grandmother has been a stellar example."

I retrieved my phone and swiped the screen.

"Harry"

"This should be good," I said to no one as I hit the green icon. "Hello."

My eldest brother's voice came through the speaker. "Ash, have you seen the breaking news?"

CHAPTER

18

Rae

"I'm glad you could meet me," Frankie said as he opened my car door.

Stepping out of the car, I felt the sea breeze whip my hair around my face. Almost immediately, I knew that the blue jeans and top I'd worn weren't enough to protect me from the cooler morning air. Goose bumps scattered over my arms. Since I'd awakened to Frankie's invitation, I hadn't had much time to dress nicer or warmer.

He had a car parked along the side of the highway and was dressed in nice pants and a button-down shirt, unbuttoned at the collar.

"Wow," I said, scanning him up and down. "You didn't tell me this was a dress-up occasion."

"It's not. I have to go into the office."

"Yeah, that work thing."

"I hate that we are on different schedules. You're off when I work, and vice versa."

Once again, Frankie and I were on the edge of Highway 1, the beach of Garrapata State Park hardly visible through the morning fog. The scene before us was eerie and beautiful at the same time. Streaks of sunshine came through the condensation like spotlights from heaven, only to be lost again in the low-lying clouds.

He tilted his head. "You haven't told me where you work."

"The truth is that I'm not sure if I want to stay."

Frankie grinned. "How do you feel about the business of wine?"

"Like a fish out of water."

"So, where is this mysterious place of employment?"

I looked down at the gravel near the side of the road before looking up. "I'm not embarrassed. I guess I didn't know you were rich."

"I'm not rich, Rae. My family is."

I pointed at the fancy car, much newer than mine. "That looks rich."

"That's a company car. My dad doesn't want me riding my bike to the office." Frankie reached for my hand. "What does my family have to do with your job?"

I took a deep breath, ripping off the Band-Aid. "I'm

working at the Cliffs. I'm a server." I held the air in my lungs, waiting for his response. Before he could answer, I spoke fast. "I thought I saw you there the other night. Maybe this" —I motioned from him to me— "isn't a good idea."

Frankie raised my hand he was holding and tilted his head. "It doesn't feel like a bad idea."

He was right. Although this was the first move he'd made, it didn't feel wrong.

I'd known Frankie since the beginning of last year at the university, and throughout time, even on our picnic and motorcycle ride, we'd kept things in the friend zone. Holding hands. Leaning against each other. Now, feeling the warmth of his touch, I looked up at his light-blue eyes. "Um."

A sweet and sexy smile curled his lips and lifted his cheeks. "How many times do I need to bring you to one of my favorite places on earth before I get to kiss you?"

"Technically, I drove myself."

He gently squeezed my hand. "My question still stands."

"Even knowing I'm a server? My family could never be members there."

"That doesn't matter to me. Hell, Rae, we're young. I refuse to be defined by my family. Yes, I'll do my time and learn what I can. I love them. That doesn't mean I want to be them or that I don't. My parents are actually decent people. I don't know where the future leads, but

I won't let where I was born or to whom define me. Don't let those things define you either."

I loved everything Frankie was saying—not only what, but how, the conviction in his voice, the warmth of his hand. Tentatively, I took a step closer.

I wasn't sure what my apprehension was about. I wasn't inexperienced or even a virgin, and this was only a kiss. Maybe my uneasiness was that I'd been thinking about all Beth had told me and considering my future move. I knew I should quit the Cliffs.

Did I give my notice to the Cliffs before I was in an uncomfortable and illegal situation based on her information, or did I wait for what she said was inevitable to occur?

I'd lain awake most of the night after Beth and I had talked, thinking about it. Thankfully, I wasn't scheduled for the club the following day or today. However, today was Thursday before the big Memorial Day rush, and beginning tomorrow, I was scheduled to work all three days, ten hours each day. We were already shorthanded.

Everyone I worked with said that the influx of out-of-state members meant a big increase in tips. Maybe if I could make it through this weekend...

Letting go of my hand, Frankie stepped even closer. The fresh scent of body wash filled my senses. His chest came within millimeters of mine, so close that a deep breath would connect us. The cool air disappeared as I tilted my chin upward and his arms came around my waist.

"Is this yes?" he asked.

I nodded with a grin.

It was yes. I wanted to be kissed by someone like Frankie.

He wasn't some disgusting man at the club, one who believed that either his position in authority or the balance in his bank account gave him the right to do whatever he wanted.

My hands went to Frankie's chest as he pulled me closer. Stretching my toes, I lifted myself until our lips connected. The second of awkwardness disappeared as he moved his hands higher on my lower back and the warmth of his kiss washed through me.

How long had it been since I'd had a boyfriend?

Too long was the answer.

When we finally pulled apart, we both smiled.

Frankie tilted his head toward the wooden stairs. "Come down to the beach with me?"

I chewed on my lower lip as I stared out at the lingering fog below. "I can't see the beach."

"It's there. I promise."

I was a step behind Frankie, halfway down the steps that were fully immersed in the fog. The sound of waves confirmed the presence of the ocean, yet it still wasn't visible. I had images from movies skirting across my consciousness. There was the one where people were crossing a rickety, old, suspension bridge when all at once a pterodactyl appeared.

Finally, we came to the sand. Once again, Frankie reached for my hand. "Isn't this cool?"

"If you mean cold, a bit," I replied with a shiver.

Letting go of my hand, he wrapped his arm around me, tucking me close to his side. Together, we walked forward until the water became visible. It was hard to describe the way it happened, as if a clouded lens focused. The fog hung heavily around the tall banks veiling the flowers, yet out on the ocean, the haze was clearing. Rays of sunlight and patches of blue sky appeared.

"This is beautiful," I said.

Frankie turned toward me and gently reached for my chin. "So are you, Rae. I want another kiss."

There was no need to answer; I simply did as I had before and pushed up on my toes. His lips met mine. Strong and soft, forceful yet yielding, I found myself lost as his hand found its way beneath my shirt. Warm fingers splayed over my lower back.

"When can I take you on a real date?" he asked. "Not the club, if you don't want to go there. Somewhere to show you that I think you're special."

"This beach is special."

"This weekend? I'm off for all three days."

I shook my head. "Work is supposed to be really busy with the holiday."

"My parents have all sorts of things planned for the

holiday weekend. Friends coming into town and parties. If not then, how about Tuesday?"

I wasn't sure if I would have to work. The schedule had posted; I just hadn't looked at it yet. And then I remembered. "Oh shit. My mom and her husband and daughter are supposed to be here tomorrow. I told them I had to work, but she said they'd be here until Tuesday."

Frankie grinned. "You just remembered your family?"

"I-I knew. I've been a little preoccupied."

Frankie reached for my hips. "I have been too, Rae. I keep thinking about you. The other night, I thought I saw you, but then you were gone."

Shit. He had seen me.

"At the Cliffs?"

His eyes opened wide. "It was you."

"It was."

My phone vibrated in my back pocket. "I guess cell service is stronger than sea fog." I swiped the screen. It was a text message from Mr. Kluser.

My pulse sped up as I assured myself this was related to the club.

"Everyone in the kitchen by eleven. Emergency."

I looked up from the screen to Frankie. "So much for my day off."

"What is it?" Frankie asked.

"Something at work." I smiled at his clothes and his leather loafers in the sand. "Don't you have to go too?"

"I do, but working for my parents has a few advantages."

"Did you tell them you had a secret date?"

"Something like that." He reached for my hand. "I guess we'll have to survive on text messages for a few more days."

CHAPTER

19

Rae

D riving back north to the country club, I felt lighter than I had in a while. After Frankie and I made it back up the stairs, he walked me to my car and we kissed goodbye. He said it wasn't goodbye because we'd be seeing each other again. Thankfully, up on the road, the fog had started to break apart.

I didn't like thinking about the fact that the guy I liked was from an uber-rich, influential family.

To me, I wanted him to be just Frankie.

Yet I liked that he wasn't fazed by my employment. Finally confessing was a weight off my shoulders that I hadn't realized I had been carrying.

Pulling into the employee parking lot, I was shocked at all the cars. The clock on my dashboard read 10:53. I'd made it with a whole seven minutes to spare. As I opened my car door, a small Nissan whipped into the space next to me, narrowly missing my door. Before I could comment, Chad lowered his passenger window. "Sorry, Goldilocks. I didn't see you opening your door."

Obviously, was the reply on the tip of my tongue. Instead, I smiled and shook my head. My day had started too well to let a simple near miss at death upset me.

"Wait up," Chad called as he closed his window and got out of the car.

I waited. "Where were you the other night? People were worried. They said you never miss."

"I didn't miss."

"You weren't there."

"There was some bullshit investigation. I was on suspension." He flashed me his one-hundred-watt smile. "I passed, I'm back." His smile faded. "Now, this. It's unreal."

"What?"

"The reason Kluser called this meeting. Fuck, it's like someone is purposely trying to hurt the club."

"What happened?"

Chad opened his eyes and gasped. "You're joking, right?"

"I'm not. What are you talking about?"

He shook his head as we entered a back entrance to the club. It was an employee-only door, leading to a back hallway that reached the locker room, Kluser's office, and into the kitchen. Before Chad answered me, voices came into range. The realization came in increments—small clues or fragments that finally painted a picture.

I saw McKenzie's shattered expression and Beth's puffy eyes. Pete was hugging Gloria. It wasn't until I turned toward Chad and watched him wipe a tear from his cheek that I had a grasp on the knowledge that something tragic had happened. Mentally, I took attendance. We were all present and accounted for.

Mr. Kluser's gaze met mine before he turned away.

I never had to tell him that I forgot to go to his office. Mr. Maze sending me to the Tertian Lounge was my alibi. There was definitely a part of me that wondered if Maze had caught Max with his pants down. I stifled a grin, knowing this wasn't the atmosphere.

Max Kluser lifted his hand. "This news should not —I repeat, should not—affect this weekend's guests or festivities. We're still planning on three busy days. Our refrigerators are packed full, and you're all scheduled to work."

I moved my gaze from person to person. Heads were shaking and fingertips were on people's lips. It seemed obvious that I was the only one who didn't know what was happening.

"What about plans? If there's a funeral—"

Mr. Kluser shook his head. "It won't be this weekend. It's an active investigation. And by the way, the beach is closed. No more after-work parties. The police found the cooler and setup. If I had my way, you'd all be docked this weekend's wages to pay for whatever alcohol you stole from the club."

Pete stepped forward. "Are we going to be questioned?"

"Regarding the theft of alcohol?"

"I meant," Pete said, "about Scarlett?"

Mr. Kluser nodded. "I would suspect. Scarlett worked here for over a year."

Scarlett.

"First, Miss Temple was found on our property, and now Scarlett."

"There's security," Monica said.

"There is, but as you know, the members appreciate anonymity. They pay generous membership fees that save them from twenty-four-seven surveillance. Scarlett was found in an area that is outside the reach of cameras. As most of you probably heard from the news, she was discovered late yesterday when her body washed up on the beach near the southern boundary of our land."

"She didn't necessarily have to be on this property," Chad said. "Couldn't she have been dropped by a boat?"

"I'm sure," Mr. Kluser said, "that the police are investigating all possibilities."

"How long has she been dead?" Beth asked.

Mr. Kluser shook his head. "Not long. I can't say anything else. It's all under investigation." He lifted his hand to stop comments. "I called you all here to get this out and over. There's nothing any one of you can do. When the doors open, our members don't want to see sad faces. They don't pay what they pay to look at tears or frowns. Get that shit out and move on. If you don't think you can do that, find someone to replace you. No sick leave or bereavement is available through this weekend. Am I clear?"

There were murmurs, but no one else spoke up.

As Mr. Kluser walked back toward his office, I pulled out my phone and clicked a local news app. My stomach twisted at the picture. I'd never met Scarlett, but all the stories I'd heard made her sound like a person full of life. Her picture was pretty. She had bright blue eyes, long blond hair, a slim yet curvy figure, and an infectious smile.

I startled as Beth reached for my arm. Her tear-streaked cheeks and bloodshot eyes turned my way. "I can't do it, Rae. Not today. I've been crying since I found out this morning. Can you please work for me?"

Inhaling, I pushed away my thoughts of quitting. "What time?"

"I'm supposed to work three until close."

I had a million reasons why I didn't want to work, but Beth was my friend and doing what one didn't want to do to help a friend was what friends did. I feigned a smile. Three o'clock would give me a little time to prepare for my incoming family, but working would also mean I'd be exhausted.

Holding all of that back, I said, "Sure, Beth."

CHAPTER

20

Henri

"Why are you calling me about this?" I asked, speaking to my sister Friday afternoon.

"I'm worried about you. I just think that this seems to have similarities to Ellen..." She hesitated. "I'm sure it's bringing back memories. I want you to know I'm here for you."

"I haven't seen the news reports." I lied. "Other people have drowned since Ellen. I don't even know who this girl was."

"She was a woman, Henri—a young woman, but a woman. She was last seen almost six months ago, around the time of Ellen's death at the Cliffs."

"Are you saying she's connected to Ellen's death? Do you think she had something to do with it? Remember, I'd left. Was this *young woman*" —I emphasized my sister's description— "near Ellen?"

"She wasn't a member," Ash said. "Her name was Scarlett. She worked there."

I leaned back in my office chair as Ashleigh continued to describe Scarlett. As she spoke, I recalled all the things my sister didn't know, things no one knew, no one but Richard and me. I remembered the panic in her eyes when she realized she was captive. At first, she believed it was a joke or an elaborate misunderstanding.

She'd even laughed it off, until she didn't.

Ashleigh knew the information the news reports said. They didn't know about her strawberry-shaped birthmark on her left ass cheek or the scar around her right ankle where she'd been chained for the first month of her captivity. They didn't know the time we'd dedicated to make Scarlett amenable to our plans.

Eventually, Scarlett came to her senses and, in doing so, gained her freedom from the shackle, but not from the suite. Privileges worked in a similar way to punishments. Pavlov was onto something.

Would the coroner be able to determine the cause of the scar on her ankle or others?

Richard was certain she'd had broken ribs after she first became our guest. We didn't get confirmation—as she wasn't tended to by a physician—and with time, they too healed. Each step along the way was a necessary evil.

My lips curled.

Sadly, it was Scarlett's eventual compliance that caused me to lose interest.

The fight she'd had was gone. Her spark fizzled. Yes, Scarlett followed the rules; she willingly fell to her knees and sucked me or spread her legs and took me wherever I desired. However, not even the prompt of punishment would elicit a visceral response.

I'd read a story once about a man who would chain animals outside, just out of reach of food and water. At first, the dogs would bark. Until they didn't, until they accepted their fate.

Scarlett had reached that point.

She no longer asked for anything or complained about anything. Even the balcony that had at one time been her reward was no longer a form of motivation.

Granted, the timing of my discontent was unfortunate, being before the holiday weekend.

I hadn't given that as much thought as getting rid of her. I could have spent another week or month with my cock in her mouth—or done as the man in the story did and stop feeding her.

I scoffed.

That was what Scarlett had become, a pet that no longer earned attention.

I hadn't recognized the extent of my ennui. Days become weeks and weeks months. My realization came when I saw the new little blonde in the Tertian Lounge.

Rae.

She'd sparked an interest deep within me.

Out with the old and in with the new.

"Henri, are you listening?"

"Sorry, Ash. I am, and I'm not. I have a meeting in fifteen minutes. The unfortunate death of some waitress will need to wait to receive my attention. Besides, what's the big deal?"

"The big deal? A person is dead."

"And as I said, people drown. It happens."

"It looks bad for Woodland Cliffs," my sister said. "Mother is concerned, as are the other families on the board. Two holidays in a row."

I scoffed. "Mother needs a new hobby. If my calendar is correct, other holidays occurred between the Harvest Gathering and the Memorial Day celebration. You may have heard of them. Let's see, there's Thanksgiving, Christmas, Hanukkah, and Kwanzaa, to name a few. Ellen's death was ruled an accident on the property. Does Mother or anyone else believe this..." —I purposely paused— "you said her name was what?"

"Scarlett. Scarlett Barrack."

"Yes, well, was she on the property?"

"No one knows. She could have been dropped off by boat farther out. They're working with the Coast Guard and discussing the currents and the tides."

"Hell, maybe she simply went swimming off a rock at Big Sur and floated. I'm not a marine expert. Do currents run north or south?"

Ashleigh was silent for a moment. "Fine, Henri. Forget I called. You're obviously not upset."

"Not about that girl. I would have liked to hear from my sister that I am going to be an uncle. Judging from the gathering at the Cliffs, my call or text was lost in cyberspace."

"I meant to tell you at lunch, but you rushed away."

"Congratulations, sis. For the kid's sake, I hope this is because you want kids and not to bring life back to a dying marriage."

"That's also why I didn't say anything. I knew you'd turn it around."

"Forgive me for pointing out the obvious," I said. "My meeting is approaching. I'll talk to you later." I hit the disconnect button on my phone without waiting for her response.

After running my palm over my face, I sat forward, placing my elbows on my desk. For the first time in months, I felt a new surge of energy circulating through me. Currently, Richard was taking care of the suite Scarlett had vacated. I'd told him to order new everything, down to the rugs and curtains. It had to be perfect for my next guest.

Grinning, I imagined her welcome to my home; the fear was addictive. I longed to see that emotion again, to feel the electricity in the air as her fate became clearer.

First, I'd begin the hunt.

Would you be missed?

Changing my computer to incognito, I accessed a well-coded VPN and began typing. "Miss Rae Watson, who are you?"

CHAPTER

21

Rae

My phone rang as I closed the door to my apartment and headed toward my car. I'd spent most of the morning cleaning and doing laundry—the fun and exciting life of a single woman on her own. I didn't hate it, but I thought that sometime in my past as I planned my future, I'd had images of glamour, spending days feasting on grapes poolside while receiving a mani-pedi. Or maybe the manicure and pedicure were part of my spa services, the ones that would, of course, include massages and skin treatments. Instead, my hands were treated with dish soap as I washed dishes, and my feasting was not on grapes, but leftover pizza from last night's delivery.

Yes, I preferred healthier, but shopping was still on my to-do list.

"Hello," I answered, seeing my mother's name on the screen.

"We're at the airport in Cleveland, Rae. Jendy is so excited to fly, and I can't wait to see you."

A small twinge of guilt twisted my stomach. "Mom, I want to see you too, but I told you this is a busy weekend at work."

"Surely, they're not making you work all weekend?"

"Technically, yeah," I said as I walked toward my car. "I even picked up a shift for tonight. I'll be free all day on Tuesday."

"Honey, we know you're busy. Maybe we can meet for breakfast? You're not expected to be at work from sunup to sundown, are you?"

Her understanding brought a smile to my face. "Breakfast would be wonderful. I could have you over here one morning. Does Jendy still love pancakes?"

"She'd eat them for breakfast, lunch, and dinner if Eric and I would let her."

I made a mental note to get pancake mix. "Sounds great."

"Tomorrow morning?" Mom asked.

A quick check of the clock on the dashboard told me I had just enough time to stop at the market on my way to the club. Even though I wouldn't receive my next paycheck until tomorrow, I was set on cash from the tips I'd earned working the Tertian Lounge.

"Tomorrow sounds good. I don't have to be at work until one. Can you all be here about nine?"

"We can. We are staying close. I can't wait to hug you," Mom said.

"Love you."

"Love you, too. I'll text when we land."

Disconnecting the call, I backed out of my parking space, making a quick list of groceries in my head. If I hurried, I'd have time to run the groceries back to the apartment and still make it to the club in plenty of time to change clothes.

With my mind on all my errands, I almost didn't see the white Chevy Sonic or the door opening until the occupant began waving. I slammed on my brakes. "Shit, Robyn."

I rolled down my window.

"Robyn, why aren't you in Long Beach?"

She walked to my window. With each step, I witnessed the sadness in her expression become more evident, as well as the weight on her shoulders. "I'm sorry, Rae. I don't know where to go. I sublet my apartment until August and, well..." Her words trailed away as she sighed. "I don't want to go to my parents and admit they were right."

"Right about what?" I asked. "Parker?"

She nodded as a tear glistened on her cheek. "If I could crash with you while I try to sort some stuff out..?"

Driving back into a parking space, I put the car in park, turned it off, and got out. Reaching for my friend, I pulled her into a hug. "Yes, of course. Warning, I'm working some long hours." We walked together up the sidewalk toward my apartment door. "And I have my mom, sister, and mom's husband coming for breakfast tomorrow."

Tears filled Robyn's eyes. "I've been driving all night, and I don't know where else to go." She closed her eyes. "I'm really tired." When she opened them again, I saw how bloodshot they were. "If I stay at a hotel, my dad will see it on my credit card statement. If he sees it, he'll tell my mom, and then I'll get a call I don't want."

I reached for her arm. "Robyn, you can stay with me as long as you need."

"I'll pay rent."

A smile curled my lips. If Robyn paid even a small portion, with my increase in tips, I might be able to quit the Cliffs...

I shook my head as we reached the door I'd just locked. "Whatever you can contribute is fine." Turning the key, I pushed the door open, happy that I'd taken some time to tidy up. Hurrying into the kitchen, I opened a cupboard and removed a key chain with one key from an inside hook. "Here is a key."

"You're the best, Rae."

Turning, I looked at the clock. "Shit. I was going to the store, but now I need to get to the Cliffs."

"Leave me a list. If I shop for you, I'll feel like I'm doing something."

"I can't ask you to do that," I said. "You just said you haven't slept."

"Rae, I asked to crash at your place. You can ask me to shop."

Nodding, I quickly scribbled out a list.

Pancake mix, eggs, turkey bacon, fresh fruit, and orange juice.

"Get anything else you want to eat," I said as I handed her the list and dug into my purse for cash. I peeled a hundred-dollar bill away from other bills and said a mental thank-you to Henri Turner. He was a creep, but he tipped well.

"I can pay for the groceries," Robyn argued.

"And your dad will see the charge. Besides, I like having disposable income, and since I'm usually working afternoons and evenings, my refrigerator is a little bare." I grinned. "Okay, it's like the old nursery rhyme, you know Mother Hubbard's cupboard?"

"At least you're not an old lady living in a shoe."

"One day, and it's going to be a Jimmy Choo or Louboutin. You wouldn't believe what I've seen at the Cliffs. Holy cow, those ladies know how to dress."

"Are you safe there?" Robyn shook her head. "I know, I know. I listen to too many crime podcasts, but on my way here, I stopped for breakfast and saw the news in the restaurant. They found another body at that country club."

"I don't know much about it, but she did use to work there. Everyone is pretty broken up."

Robyn reached forward and pulled me close into a hug. "Thank you."

When we separated, I took her hands in mine. "You're welcome to stay here as long as you need. And although I need to run, I'm all ears if you need to talk."

"Thank you."

As I drove away, I had new questions racing through my mind.

What had happened between Robyn and Parker, and why did she come back after only a few weeks?

I had no qualms about taking her in. She was my friend. That's what friends did.

What if someone had taken Scarlett in when she needed it?

Had she needed that?

Had she told a friend what was happening?

Where had she been for the last six months?

So many questions.

CHAPTER

22

Rae

Adjusting my skirt and coming out of the locker room with my myriad of thoughts swirling around my head, I almost collided with Mr. Kluser. My feet stilled as I fought to balance and not to wobble on the high heels. "Oh, Mr. Kluser, I'm sorry."

His eyes narrowed as he scanned me from my head to my toes. He nodded. "Thanks, Watson. It's a good thing we have you and a few others who didn't know Scarlett. It's in your hands to keep the members happy."

I let out a breath, thankful he didn't mention the other night and my lack of attendance in his office. "It's still sad."

"Don't get emotional now. We have too much work for that."

I tilted my head. "But you are upset, aren't you?"

He inhaled and stood straighter. "She was a good kid. I have memories like everyone else. No matter what anyone thought of her, Scarlett was too young to end up floating on the shores of the Cliffs." His gaze narrowed. "I don't recall seeing you on the schedule for tonight."

"Beth was pretty upset. She asked me to cover."

"You can't cover the whole weekend. Beth better get her shit together." He looked past me to the kitchen. "They all need to. Now, keep a smile on your face, Watson. Your willingness to pitch in hasn't gone unnoticed. Beth was supposed to be a server. I sure as hell don't want you filling that role for the first time now."

"I can handle it," I said confidently. "I was a server for years at Applebee's and Texas Roadhouse."

He scoffed. "Apples and oranges. Woodland Cliffs is not even similar to those establishments. This is a five-star country club with VIP members." He called Chad over. "Keep an eye on Watson. She can start out serving, but if she gets bogged down, I want you and McKenzie to take her tables and she can go back to bussing."

Chad turned my way and winked. "My eye is on you, Goldilocks."

"Goldilocks?" Mr. Kluser repeated in question.

"Something my dad used to call me. Watson is fine."

Mr. Kluser chuckled as he turned toward his office, mumbling, "Goldilocks."

"Thanks a lot," I said as I punched Chad's arm.

"Sorry, but honestly, we all need to smile."

"Any words of wisdom for serving here? Apparently, my experience is more like slumming it to Kluser. I don't think he has much faith."

"Don't sweat it. He likes to think he's running the Taj Mahal or maybe Key Largo."

"The island?"

Chad laughed. "You're smart. Most people think it's a private club in Florida."

Before I could respond, we were both staring up at the table assignments for the servers. "Do you know the table numbers?" Chad asked.

"Yep." I did. After the first night when Kluser made a big deal about it, I decided to learn them backward and forward.

I reached for one of the electronic tablets. With it, the server—me—could take orders and simultaneously send them to the kitchen and the bar. Admittedly, it was better technology than I'd had when I'd worked at the other restaurants. I assumed those establishments had made improvements over time, but in the meantime, I could handle this.

"I can't log on," I said under my breath, no longer completely confident in my ability.

Shit.

Task one—failed.

"It's because you don't have a number to be a server," McKenzie said, reaching for the tablet in my hand. "I'd tell you to use mine, but if you screw up, I don't want it on my number."

"Thanks for the confidence."

She grinned, giving me back the tablet. "Telling the truth."

Yeah, I'm not Scarlett.

While those words were on the tip of my tongue, I decided against saying them. I might not be the server she was, but I was alive, so there was that.

McKenzie tilted her head toward the hallway. "Go talk to Max. He can set you up with a number."

I didn't mean for my expression to change, but it must have. McKenzie stepped in front of me. "Tell him the doors are open and your tables are filling." No words came to mind as stories from Beth filled my thoughts. McKenzie forced a smile. "Come on, Rae, I'll go with you."

"But your tables..?"

"They'll get waited on as soon as Max sets up your number."

Her unexpected assistance was welcome, as well as the use of my name. "Thank you."

My mom was a firm believer in karma. Maybe a good deed for Robyn earned me a good deed in return.

McKenzie knocked on Mr. Kluser's door.

"Come in," he bellowed from inside.

The office was exactly as I remembered it, and it in no way represented the arrogance he tried to portray. His gaze went from McKenzie to me and back to her.

McKenzie spoke first, "Rae needs a number to get into the ordering system."

"Go on, McKenzie. The doors are open."

"Yeah, and I'm going to help Rae." She reached again for the tablet in my hand and handed it across his desk.

For only a moment, it seemed as if unspoken words were flying. Maybe it was my imagination. I'd spent way too much time thinking about Beth's warnings. I could be misconstruing a simple exchange.

With an exaggerated exhale, Mr. Kluser took the tablet and began hitting keys on his computer. McKenzie and I stood shoulder to shoulder until he opened the tablet and then handed it toward me. "You're 0419. Don't forget it."

I could remember that. Nodding, I reached for the tablet.

"Why would you give her that number?" McKenzie asked. "It was Scarlett's."

Mr. Kluser nodded toward his computer screen. "It's Miss Watson's birthday—month and day." His brow furrowed. "Interesting coincidence, born on the same day as Scarlett. Now, get to work."

My stomach twisted.

"Thank you," I said as we left his office.

"That's some freaky coincidence," McKenzie said as we headed toward the kitchen. "Is that really your birthday?"

"It is. How old was she?" As soon as I said it, I recalled the story I'd read. "Twenty-four. I remember now. Three years older than me."

"Too young," McKenzie said as we passed through the swinging door.

The din of members filled the room as sun streamed beyond the large windows overlooking the Pacific Ocean. Other servers were fluttering about, including Chad. His gaze met mine, and he grinned.

"You've got this, Rae. But if you have a question, let one of us know."

"Thanks for being nice," I said with a sigh.

"You like me, remember?" He grinned. "Listen, I'm not nice. I just don't want to deal with shit."

"Noted." I opened my tablet. Next to the table number was a list of names, a cheat sheet of sorts. The names were to make it appear that we knew each and every person who entered the door. Perhaps it was that these people were so important—or thought they were —that they were meant to be identified by name.

As I walked toward table twelve, I read the name: Hamilton.

Shit.

My gaze fluttered to the table and back to the screen. Hamilton: Mitchell. Audrey.

This wasn't the best way to meet Frankie's parents,

but hopefully I could do it without spilling something on them. I pasted on my biggest smile.

"Hello, Mr. and Mrs. Hamilton. I'm Rae, and I'm going to be taking care of you today."

CHAPTER

23

Bernie Maze

Inhaling, I opened the door to the executive conference room and made my way to the head of the table. Currently, the eight chairs were empty, but that welcome silence wouldn't last long. As soon as I'd heard the news about Scarlett Barrack, I'd known it would come to this.

Hell, even if she'd been found dead somewhere else, possibly hundreds of miles away, there would still be blowback on the club. After all, she'd been an employee, and Woodland Cliffs Country Club was one of the last places she was seen.

Having her battered body end up on our shore was like a damn neon sign that refused to lose power. Making matters worse, her body showed up on one of our busiest weekends of the year. Fucking sign had an arrow pointing at us.

I laid the folder of information I had on Miss

Barrack on the long glass table and walked to the windows. Despite the storm brewing and about to lightning and thunder within this room, everything else was in order for our three-day celebration. The sun was shining outside, and temperatures were forecast in the high sixties. No signs of rain. The swimming pools were heated, tennis courts freshly painted, and the golf course was manicured to perfection. We were almost at full staff, with strict directions that no one could take time off. The restaurants and bars were fully stocked.

My stomach twisted as my attention went back to the manila folder.

"Maze."

I turned in time to see Lowell Holmes and Warren Harris enter the conference room. "Gentlemen."

Warren's head was shaking. "Awful, just awful."

"How many memberships have we lost?" Lowell asked.

"Have a seat, gentlemen. The rest of the board is on their way."

As they took a seat, Wilma Turner and her daughter, Ashleigh Maxwell, entered. Whatever they'd been discussing between themselves faded away as Wilma took the chair at the far end of the table with a nod to Mr. Holmes and Mr. Harris. Theodore and Amelia Cannon were a few moments behind. The last people to enter were Jared Oliver and Mitchell Hamilton.

"My wife is waiting downstairs," Mr. Hamilton said.

I nodded. If he was asking how long this would take, I didn't have an answer.

"The Bowens are out of town," I began, still standing. "I spoke with Clark on the phone before coming here. He and Anita are up to speed on everything that's happening."

"I'm not," Wilma Turner said. "I certainly hope you can tell us more than the local news." She shook her head. "It's all about sensationalizing tragedy for them."

"A girl is dead," Ashleigh Maxwell snapped. "That is a tragedy."

I walked to the door and closed us in.

Speaking to the room, I addressed my comment to Mrs. Maxwell as I made my way back to my seat. "You're right, Mrs. Maxwell. It's a tragedy." I looked at Mr. Holmes. "As to your earlier question regarding membership, as you know, we had two prominent families opt not to renew their membership after the incident last autumn." I did my best not to look at the Turners as I spoke. "As for this situation, no one has called to let us know they want to cancel their membership." I exhaled as I sat. "We have, however, received multiple cancellations for reservations this weekend, either in the restaurant or with activities."

"More than normal?" Mrs. Cannon asked.

"I would need to go back to the last few Memorial Day weekends and compare." I ran my finger down the edge of the folder, debating how much I could share. "I spoke to Sheriff Strong earlier today. He wanted me to close the club, claiming it was a possible crime scene."

"Close it?" Murmurs bloomed like a mushroom cloud, growing louder.

I waited for the comments to quiet. "As you saw when you drove up, we're open and will remain open. The Woodland Sheriff's Department did a sweep last night into this morning and determined that Miss Barrack washed ashore. There's no evidence to support the hypothesis that she died on our property. There also is no evidence that she was killed. Her death still may be ruled an accident."

"I heard on the news," Mr. Holmes said, "that the coroner is still trying to determine time of death." He shrugged. "At first, I wondered if she'd been deceased since she was last seen, six months ago."

I shook my head. "No, Miss Barrack was recently alive. That's why law enforcement wants to keep information limited. They're hoping—I believe—to get more facts regarding her recent whereabouts."

"I heard she'd been injured," Mrs. Maxwell said.

"She is dead," her mother replied.

"I heard that the body showed signs of injuries premortem, such as possible broken bones that had healed."

Mrs. Cannon's eyes grew wide. "Are you suggesting that the poor girl was tortured?"

"Mrs. Maxwell," I said, "it's best not to speculate."

Mr. Harris spoke up. "My wife and I allow our

children to roam these grounds. Our oldest daughter is fifteen. Are we concerned that there may be some kind of sicko at this club who tortured that girl and then killed her?"

"My granddaughter is sixteen," Mrs. Cannon said.

"Mine is fifteen, and she's spending the weekend here with us."

"Maybe they should not come—"

"No, no," I interrupted, raising my voice. "This is why I called you all together. We need a united front. You're not only members of the executive board, but also representatives of this country club. It's imperative that you don't alter your plans and, if asked, you minimize the club's involvement in this sad incident. The young woman may have fallen from a boat, or sadly, she may have decided to take her own life. We can't let vicious rumors be perpetuated."

"Are you saying it's better for us to foster victim blaming than recognize that we may have a dangerous individual among us?" Mr. Oliver asked.

"No," I said, "no one is victim blaming. I'm saying we don't have enough evidence."

"Maybe whoever pushed Ellen did this too," Mrs. Cannon proposed.

"Unfortunately, Ellen Temple fell. It was an accident," Mrs. Turner said matter-of-factly.

"How many accidents need to happen here before we face the possibility of something more nefarious?" Mr. Harris asked before turning to me. "Have there been new hires, possibly around the time of the Harvest Gathering? I think the club needs to do a thorough background check on every person who is employed here."

"I agree," Mrs. Maxwell said.

Heads nodded around the table.

"I assure you," I said, "that every employee is given a thorough background check. The police have all their information."

"I'm going to say it," Mr. Oliver said. "What about members?"

"Are you suggesting it's a member who is responsible?" Mrs. Turner asked.

"I'm suggesting that no one is above suspicion," he replied.

"The best scenario for the club is a sad string of accidents," I interjected. "When I spoke to Mr. and Mrs. Bowen earlier, Mrs. Bowen suggested that we be proactive. Miss Barrack had no close family. A cousin called in saying she hadn't heard from Scarlett. That cousin lives in North Carolina. Mrs. Bowen suggested that Woodland Cliffs donate the money for Miss Barrack's funeral and burial costs as well as consider something to remember her, perhaps a scholarship for employees."

Heads around the table again nodded.

"Can I count on everyone here to support that decision and to support Woodland Cliffs, not only this weekend but in the future?"

CHAPTER

24

Ashleigh

"I'm sure we can get a table at this time of the afternoon," I said to Mother as we rode the country club's elevator to the first floor.

I wouldn't normally take an elevator one level, but it was here for members such as my mother and Lowell Holmes.

"Would you like to join us, Mr. Holmes?"

"Aren't you kind, Ashleigh. I can't imagine anything nicer than to have a midafternoon snack and drink with two lovely women."

It was hard not to notice the way he was looking at my mother. It was kind of cute, watching a man in his seventies flirt. Lowell Holmes had lost his wife last year. It was clear that he was ready to move on, or maybe he was lonely. After all, his children lived thousands of miles away. Even though my father had passed seven years ago, by the way my mother's lips pursed, she wasn't in the market for company.

"We'd be happy to have you," I said, filling the awkward silence as the elevator came to a stop.

"Wilma?" Lowell asked.

"As long as you don't get the last piece of chocolate mousse pie, you're welcome to join us."

Lowell's face reddened as his laugh jiggled his stomach. He continued to chat as we made our way to the hostess stand and asked for a table.

"Of course, Mrs. Maxwell," the hostess said as she looked down at an electronic tablet. "We have a table near the window."

"Hmm."

Ignoring my mother's hum, I thanked the young girl and told her that would be lovely.

Lowell pulled out a chair for my mother. I couldn't decide what was more fun, watching him flirt or her annoyance. They were both more enjoyable than thinking about the unfortunate young lady who had died. The information I had received about her injuries came secondhand from my brother Harrison. I had no reason to doubt his sources, and the premise had me more than a little concerned.

Was there a monster on the loose?

Was Woodland Cliffs the hunting ground?

Were we prey?

"Is Chad Jackson working?" my mother asked the hostess, her question quelling mine. "Oh," she went on,

"I suppose I should have asked before we were seated. He can wait on us."

"I'm sorry, Mrs. Turner. Chad isn't here today."

My mother's eyes met mine.

"It will be fine," I reassured her.

"You're in Rae's section," the hostess said. "If you'd prefer someone else..."

"Rae will be just fine," I answered before my mother could turn the choice of server into a full-on interview process. I turned to Mother. "We're having a snack. We'll be fine."

The hostess nodded. "I'll let her know you're here."

I read her name tag. "Thank you, Monica."

"Chad is a fine fellow," Lowell said as he reached for his napkin. "But it makes me think."

"About?" Mother asked.

"Please don't take this as a chauvinistic statement."

I straightened my neck as the small hairs on my neck jumped to attention. Preambles such as that always made me bristle. It was as if someone were seeking approval for their upcoming sexist statement.

Lowell leaned forward and lowered his voice. "It doesn't seem to me that a female would hurt another female."

"It happens," I said.

"But not like that Scarlett was hurt."

I shook my head. "We don't know for sure. My information wasn't firsthand."

"Mine either," he said, "but it matches up. And it

has me thinking about the male employees, such as Chad."

Mother shook her head. "Ridiculous. Chad wouldn't do that. Poor boy. Bernie Maze called me about him the other day. Ridiculous. Rumors."

"What rumors? How do you know he wouldn't?" I asked.

"Hello."

We all turned to the blonde with soft brown eyes, wearing the club's emblem. "Hello," I replied.

"Welcome, Mrs. Turner, Mrs. Maxwell, and Mr. Holmes. As Monica told you, my name is Rae, and I'll be your server today. Would you like a drink to start your meal?"

"Are you new?" Lowell asked.

Her cheeks filled with pink. "I am newer than most."

"Did you know Miss Barrack?"

"Miss Barrack?" she said, repeating Lowell's question. Her eyes widened. "You mean Scarlett."

"He means Miss Barrack, dear," Mother said. "It's impolite to speak of the deceased by their first name."

Rae stood taller. "I'm sorry. I didn't know her. I've heard many nice things and am very sad to hear the news."

"Coffee, two creams," Mother said.

"Gin and tonic for me, sweetheart," Lowell said.

If it was impolite to speak of the deceased in a familiar address, calling this woman sweetheart was also impolite. "Rae," I said, "I'd like a raspberry lemonade and a water."

She nodded. "I'll be back with three waters and your drinks. Is there anything else?"

"Don't waste water. I don't want one," my mother replied. "Lowell, do you?"

"No." He winked at Rae. "But keep the gin and tonics coming."

"Of course," Rae replied. "One water for you, Mrs. Maxwell, and I'll be right back."

CHAPTER

25

Rae

"Oh my God," Pete exclaimed as I entered the kitchen through the swinging door. "You drew the short straw. I'm sorry."

My eyes widened. "How does Chad put up with that lady? I haven't even taken her order and she's corrected me a dozen times."

Pete laughed. "Oh, give her time. Nothing will be right."

"Her daughter seems nice." I was doing as I'd been prompted and learning the relationships of different members.

"She can be."

"Watson," Mr. Kluser said, "you have more than one table, but at that one table are three members of the executive board. Don't screw up."

I scoffed at the added pressure as I filled a glass with ice and water, a cup with fresh coffee, and poured another glass of raspberry lemonade. The gin and tonic order was sent electronically to the bar. I'd pick it up after I delivered these.

Thankfully, as I delivered the drinks, the three board members were involved in a conversation. It was as I turned to get Mr. Holmes's gin and tonic that Mrs. Turner spoke to me as she stirred cream into her coffee.

"Dear, this is decaffeinated, right?"

"No, I'm sorry."

With a huff, she leaned back away from the table. "Take it away. If I drink caffeine at this time of day, I'll be up all night." She shook her head as I reached for the cup and saucer. "Is Chad coming in soon?"

"Mother," Mrs. Maxwell said, "you didn't ask for decaf."

I wanted to hug her. Mrs. Maxwell was right; her mother hadn't asked for decaf. "It's no problem," I said with a smile. "I'll be right back with decaffeinated coffee and your drink, Mr. Holmes."

"I shouldn't have to ask. It's her job," Mrs. Turner said as I walked away, both of us wishing Chad would materialize out of thin air.

I remembered Chad saying he'd received a large tip from Mrs. Turner. Five hundred dollars came to mind. I didn't see that in my future.

In no time, I had my problem table happy and their orders for pie sent to the kitchen. I also checked on my other tables and refilled some coffees, iced teas, and was on my way to the bar for a glass of cabernet.

With the stem in my hand, I turned, finding myself face-to-face with Mrs. Maxwell. I quickly took a step backward, silently cussing the high heels and hoping the wine didn't splash on either one of us.

"Mrs. Maxwell, may I help you?"

"First, I apologize for my mother. She's crankier than usual."

I shook my head. "No problem. Everyone is tense after Scarlett—I mean Miss Barrack."

She grinned. "I wondered if I could speak to you for a moment."

My gaze went back over the floor. Other than delivering the wine, I seemed to be caught up for now. "May I deliver this first?"

"Of course, I'll be in the hallway."

I tugged on my lower lip as I contemplated the hallway. I wasn't supposed to leave the floor, but then again, this was Mrs. Maxwell—Turner-Maxwell. Once my hands were free, I went to the side doors, and after looking for Mr. Kluser and not seeing him, I slipped into the hallway.

"I won't keep you long," she said. "First, please take this as an apology." She handed me a folded bill. I couldn't see the denomination.

"You don't need to..."

"I insist."

"Thank you." I placed the folded bill in my apron pocket.

"I'm concerned about what has happened here

lately, and well, you're new, so can you tell me if you have had any feelings regarding either employees or members?"

"Feelings?"

"Uncomfortable," she said with a tilt of her head. "I've found that women can be intuitive and sense things. Have any of your fellow employees made you uncomfortable? Are there any creeps that frequent the club?"

I smiled because, yes, I'd had that feeling. There was Chad, at first, but he has turned out to be a good guy. Then Mr. Kluser, but mentioning him would probably result in my firing. There was Beth's story about Mr. Maze and then the guy in the Tertian Lounge. Oh yeah, he was Mrs. Maxwell's brother. I shook my head. "No, nothing I can think of. Why?"

"As I said, I'm concerned. And as a member of the executive board and because my parents helped found this club, I would like to know that everyone, members and employees, is safe here."

"You're nice."

A smile curled her lips. "Not always, Rae. I can kick ass at the office, but I'm also a fixer, and when I'm with certain members of my family, I often feel the need to soften their rough edges. I also do care about the Cliffs and want it to stay a safe and enjoyable place for people to work and play." She reached out to my hand and placed a business card in my grasp. "If you think of anything, please don't hesitate to call."

I looked down at the embossed card.

Ashleigh Turner-Maxwell
Turner Industries
Vice President Internal Relations

"I guess this is what you do?"

"Not exactly, but I do care."

"That's really good to know." I looked at the closed doors. "I need to get back in there." I lifted the electronic tablet from my apron pocket. "Your pie is up."

"Then, by all means."

It wasn't until the last table emptied at 10:40 that I had a chance to kick off my shoes. I'd done as Beth said and written my name on the bottoms. We had the dining room cleaned and turned, ready for tomorrow, and fresh flowers in record time. However, Kluser wasn't there with his stopwatch.

"I guess that means no shots," Pete said as the women went to the pile of shoes.

Once in the locker room, I finally checked my phone. As people around me changed out of their work clothes, I read the messages from my mom. With each one, I felt that twinge of guilt grow, the one caused by me working instead of meeting my family at the airport. Basically, she, Jendy, and Eric were at their hotel. They took Jendy to the beach, and she loved it. They were looking forward to breakfast in the morning.

I had another message from Robyn.

Robyn.

I'd forgotten about my new roommate.

"I'm going to sleep on the sofa. Sorry to cramp your style. Some guy came by and left flowers on the porch. No card. Weird, but cute gesture. See you in the morning. I bought everything on the list. Your change is on the kitchen counter. Good night. Thank you for being so great."

Flowers?

Were they from Frankie? Why wouldn't he leave a card?

Then again, Robyn knew Frankie from classes. She wouldn't call him some guy. Maybe the guy was a delivery person. While the mystery piqued my interest, I was too tired to concentrate on it. Closing my eyes, I leaned against my locker, making a mental note to tell Robyn she could sleep in my bed. It was king-size with plenty of room for both of us.

A quick look at the time told me it was probably too late for tonight's sleeping arrangements. Robyn was most likely asleep. For only a few seconds, I wondered if it was possible to fall asleep standing up. Being as the beach parties were indefinitely canceled, maybe sleeping in the locker room would save me time.

"Hey Rae, Kluser is looking for you," Monica said.

Shit.

Now I'm awake.

CHAPTER

26

Henri

"It's too soon," Richard said as he opened the door to the now-empty suite.

My hands were on the wall beside the open glass door as I stared out at the ocean. "Scarlett loved the ocean. I think her burial at sea was appropriate." I turned back to my trusted man. "Don't you, Richard?"

"I should have checked the tides and currents better, sir. Having her wash ashore near the country club has made this worse."

"Come out here with me." I stepped onto the balcony. The breeze grew stronger with each step toward the railing. Turning, I saw Richard in the doorway. My question was direct. "Did you fuck her?"

He took a half step back and straightened his neck. "She didn't belong to me."

"Possession is nine-tenths." I turned, leaning my

ass against the railing and crossing my arms over my chest. "That leaves a tenth." When he didn't respond, I added, "I'd been suspecting it for a while."

Richard balled his hands at his sides. "Did she say anything?"

"What difference would it make now? She's gone." My voice held no emotion about her loss. It wasn't a ruse. Scarlett had become a bore, a dying dog not even willing to bark to save its own life. The time had come. I was ready to move on.

"It was her." He took a deep breath. "Wearing next to nothing, she tried to manipulate me."

I scoffed. "Her options for clothing were limited."

"She approached me."

Nodding, I said, "Your answer would then be yes." When Richard didn't respond, I went on. "Was she the first?"

His eyes narrowed. "I never touched Ellen."

The response made me laugh. "I didn't think you had. Ellen wasn't like the others. She was supposed to be more." I shrugged. She, too, was a disappointment. "And if you had, you'd be the one out to sea." I pivoted back toward the ocean and lifted my face to the breeze. "We need an understanding, Richard."

"Sir?"

"With the new one...we could train her from the beginning to take both of us."

Richard was now at my side. "Sir."

"If you and I come to an agreement, her opinion will be moot. She'll have no choice but to agree."

I watched Richard from the corner of my eye as he leaned forward and gripped the railing. In essence, I needed Richard's help. He tended to the women when I was away. Hell, he tended to them more than I did. I wasn't a caretaker, and I didn't acquire them to fulfill some knight-in-shining armor fetish. No, they served a purpose.

"I'm still in charge," I said.

That was what the women like Scarlett did; they accepted and acquiesced to my power. I was ultimately in control of every aspect of their lives. Richard might bring them their food and even provide some kind of connection. I didn't need or want that. I wanted what Scarlett had lost, that visible edge of terror in her eyes, that incomprehensible reckoning that only I could grant continued life.

Even Ellen had that look—the fire in her eyes.

Unfortunately, it wasn't until her edge was literal.

The metaphorical edge was what made me hard. Fear was such an enticing emotion. It crackled like lightning in their eyes, emanated in a sweet scent from their pores, and propelled their actions. It was a stimulus that demanded obedience, a threat that punished defiance, and a promise that lingered beneath the surface, keeping them on edge.

Losing that edge was ultimately Scarlett's undoing.

Richard hadn't said a word since my declaration.

Patting his back, I grinned. "It's okay, good man. We can share the new one too. Wait until you see her."

Richard gripped the railing and looked down to the rocks below. "I still think it's too soon. Especially if she works at the club."

"No one will miss her. She's new. She decided to move on." I grinned. "This is the time—three weeks. It's when most of the girls decide to leave or are helped. Remember Debbie?" She agreed to work a private party. That party lasted for six or seven months.

I couldn't recall.

I shifted my focus out to the water. "I've done some research on Rae. She's from the Midwest, graduated high school from some small town in Ohio. Her father died when she was a teenager. When her mother remarried, Rae moved out here to go to college and get a new life."

Richard nodded. "No close family is a plus."

"She lives alone," I said. "I went there today."

Richard turned his eyes to me. "What? Sir, that's risky."

My cock twitched beneath my boxer briefs. The planning in cases such as this was an integral element in success. "I wanted to see where she lived," I explained. "I dropped off a delivery outside her door and watched her through the window. I'm sure she's working this weekend. The club runs their staff ragged over these holiday weekends."

"And you want to go back to her place?"

I did and I didn't.

The urge to cut this process short and move forward was growing each time I saw Rae's round tits and ass at the club. I'd made a request, in a roundabout way, to have Rae in the Tertian Lounge. There was no doubt her presence was easing my discomfort with the country club. Besides, my last name has its perks. I didn't mind using them.

I shook my head. "I don't want to wait for what we did last time."

We'd taken more time with Scarlett, trying for something different. "Remember the cameras we had at Scarlett's?" I closed my eyes and lifted my chin to the breeze. "Fuck, I've imagined Rae the same way, in her bed, naked, with her toned legs spread and her fingers pleasuring herself. This time, it won't be at her apartment, but here. I sense it, Richard. Don't you feel the excitement?" I turned toward the suite. "Is the new furniture ordered?"

"Yes, sir. It will be here Tuesday. You know, I think about Miss Ellen."

I took a step toward him. "Don't."

"She was..." Richard didn't finish the sentence.

"What? She was my fiancée?"

"I was going to say that Miss Ellen was special. She loved you."

"No, she loved who she thought I was. She loved my name and the power and money that accompany it. I tried to introduce her to some of my desires." I shook my head. "She said I needed help and threatened to tell her father or my mother. Hell, the night she slipped, before her unfortunate accident, she'd told me she was going to talk to Harry."

"Do you think she did?"

"No. I know she didn't. I never let her out of my sight that night, not until she went over the edge."

Richard swallowed, his Adam's apple bobbing. "I lied for you that night."

I patted his shoulder. "You're a good man, Richard. You deserve to have your turn with Rae, too. It's as if we're cementing our commitment to keeping this desire of mine—of ours," I corrected, "clandestine."

"I liked Scarlett."

His comment made me laugh. "Don't sweat it. Think of them like pets, not even the furry kind. No, they're more like goldfish." I looked around the room, seeing the cameras in the corners and knowing soon I'd have my new fish secured in its bowl and at my disposal. "It's best not to get too attached. And the good news is that there is always a new one to replace the old."

"I keep thinking about what Scarlett said when she knew her time was done."

"She said a lot. I don't recall anything in particular."

Richard ran his hand over his face, before his stare came my way. "She thought she was pregnant."

That wasn't possible.

"It was a lie, a ploy for sympathy. Besides, she had an implant." I snapped my fingers. "We need to learn Rae Watson's medical history. If she's not on birth control, I have a friend who can get me pills."

"Those are difficult to monitor. Debbie lied about them."

I let out a deep breath. "Debbie was desperate. She knew I was getting serious with Ellen, and she was smart—hell, smarter than Scarlett. Debbie saw the writing on the wall. Stupid Scarlett didn't grasp her fate until the knife was at her throat."

"A week, sir. Let the holiday pass and things quiet down about Scarlett."

"No more mentioning her name," I said, "or Debbie or Joyce or even Ellen. You know I trust you, man."

"I know, sir."

CHAPTER

27

Rae

"There was waves," Jendy said with a mouthful of pancakes.

My little sister made me grin. "There are."

"Go too, please?" Her little-girl sentences were missing a few words; nevertheless, I couldn't believe how much more she was talking since the last time I'd been back in Ohio.

My gaze caught my mother's as I shook my head.

Mom reached out and ran her hand over Jendy's light-colored hair. "Honey, Rae can't go today. But we get to see her now for pancakes."

My little sister grinned as she stabbed another bite of pancakes, the syrup dripping as she lifted it toward her lips. Mom asked Eric for a wet paper towel, and together, they tried to lessen the sweet mess that was slowly covering Jendy's hands and face.

It was an odd feeling, watching my mom with a man who wasn't my dad. It made me happy and sad at the same time. I missed Dad, but I saw my mom for who she was—a loving, vibrant woman. Dad wouldn't have wanted her to stop living, and now, with Eric and Jendy, she had a second chance at happiness.

Maybe it was what happened to Scarlett. It was sad, but it was also enlightening. No one deserved to be unhappy. In this moment, three years too late, I decided that my mom's happiness was something I wanted.

"I can go to the beach with you on Tuesday before you leave." I looked at Mom and Eric. "I'm sorry I'm working so much. It's a crazy time."

Robyn entered the kitchen in shorts and a t-shirt with a towel around her hair.

"Help yourself to pancakes," I said. "I think I made too many."

"Hello, Mr. and Mrs. Cole."

My mother shook her head. "Call us Jill and Eric. It's always good to see you, Robyn. You know, every time I see you two girls together, I'm struck by how similar you look."

Robyn's gaze met mine, and we smiled.

"Really?" she asked. "I am taller."

The resemblance wasn't as pronounced from our point of view, but that wasn't to say we hadn't had some fun with it at campus parties when we'd shared an apartment our freshman year.

"And my hair is longer," I added. "Wait! Is there a confession you want to make, Mom? Are we twins separated at birth?"

Mom wrapped her arm around Robyn's shoulder. "I'd claim you in a second, but I'm most certain I only had one baby at a time. It's hard to forget something like that."

She looked at the vase with the arrangement of roses. Yes, they weren't just flowers, as Robyn had called them, but long-stemmed red roses. "Who received the flowers? Was it you, Robyn?"

"No. They're for Rae."

Mom's eyes opened wide. "Is there someone you haven't mentioned?"

"His name is Frankie," Robyn volunteered. I had gotten her up-to-date on whatever it was Frankie and I were doing. "He's in some of Rae's classes, and this summer, he's making his move."

"His move?" Mom asked, lifting her eyebrows.

I shook my head. "Nothing, really." I shrugged. "He's nice. I'm not sure we're right for each other."

"Rae's just concerned," Robyn went on, "because he's a member of the fancy country club where she works."

As Mom poured herself more coffee, Eric lowered his voice. "Rae, we saw the news at the hotel last night. They mentioned the Cliffs. Isn't that the name of the country club where you work?"

"It is," I said with a sigh, unsure if I was thankful for the change in subject.

My stepfather was a cop, a detective, and as he looked at me, I saw his policeman wheels turning in his head.

"I did a bit of research," he went on, "and there was another unexplained incident at the Cliffs last fall. Do you know if they're looking into any connection?"

I shook my head. "I really have no idea what the police are doing. I'm too busy with club members to give it much thought."

"Honey," Mom said, "maybe that isn't the best place to work."

I had a list of reasons why Woodland Cliffs Country Club wasn't a good place to work, but the growing amount of cash from tips made it hard to concentrate on the negatives. "I'm only summer help. Once classes start, I need a less-demanding schedule." I scoffed. "Who would have thought I would think of the grocery as less demanding?"

Robyn made her way to the table with her breakfast. "I'm going back to the day care. I called them yesterday, and with school out, they could use my help. Maybe you could work there?"

"Oh," Mom said, "you're so good with children."

I took a long drink of my water and reminded myself that these people, the ones right here, were trying to help. The funny—odd—part was they were trying to lure me away from the club, and I hadn't told them the real reason I wanted to quit.

It wasn't the strange incidents of unexplained deaths.

It was what Beth had talked about.

That reminded me of last night, when I was told that Mr. Kluser was looking for me. I contemplated leaving without seeing him, but instead, I decided I needed to face him. I doubted that with all that was happening and the busy weekend ahead, he'd fire me on the spot.

As it turned out, nothing happened.

There was no scene with his pants around his ankles or even an uncomfortable confrontation. He wanted me to know that I'd been requested back in the Tertian Lounge and would be assigned there Friday and maybe additional days.

The only thing I said was *thank you.*

It wasn't until I was driving home that I wondered who had requested me. And then I thought about the tips. Mr. Turner's was the biggest, but the gross for the one night was more than I would make on my paycheck, even with the extra hours.

"Just keep your eyes open," Eric said. "I've found many times that people see or feel danger before it actually registers, before it's too late."

"I worry about you," Mom said.

Eric smiled as he sipped his coffee. "Rae is a smart girl. I know she'll do what she feels is right."

I lifted my coffee mug to my lips, hiding my uncertain expression.

Was I doing what was right, or was I selling out?

I supposed that time would tell.

CHAPTER

28

Rae

"You're going to the Tertian Lounge again?" Beth asked.

We were both in the locker room, changing into our black skirts, white blouses, and stupid high heels. Being close to four, most of the locker room was empty. The others were already working, having come in earlier. The schedules all varied in an effort to keep every aspect of the country club well-staffed.

I'd spent my entire shift in the gentlemen's lounge last night and walked away with over seven hundred dollars in tips. I'd been too busy to do as Eric recommended and watch. The lounge was hopping from the moment I arrived. At some points, it was standing room only. I saw and talked to members I'd only heard of or seen on television or in magazines.

Keeping the names straight in the lounge wasn't as easy as when they were seated at tables.

"It's been crazy," I said with a smile.

"Hmm."

"Beth, I don't know why they have me up there instead of you."

As she buttoned her shirt, her green eyes peered up through her lashes, coming my direction. "You did it, didn't you?"

"Did what?" I asked, my mind on getting up to the lounge.

Beth's lips came together as she tilted her head. "Max or Bernie?"

"Wait. What?" The realization hit. "No, Beth, I didn't, and I haven't been approached either. Maybe that was his intent the day Mr. Maze came down here." I lowered my voice. "Maybe Maze did catch him with his pants down." I scrunched my nose at the unwanted visual in my head. "And then McKenzie went with me on Thursday when he had to program a number into a tablet for me to be a server, which he didn't think I could do."

"He didn't?"

"No," I said, "but I made it. And now, I'm headed back upstairs." I let out a long breath. "Seriously, Beth, I'm sorry if you think I've taken this assignment from you. I didn't do it intentionally."

Beth shook her head and forced a grin. "I'm sorry, Rae. I'm just getting sick of this place and the damn politics. It seems that playing by their rules doesn't work either. Look at Scarlett. Hell, I'd quit if I could make this kind of money somewhere else." She laughed. "I've thought about a strip club, but nah. I may bend to the rules here, but that's a step I'm not willing to take."

Beth's earlier words were running laps through my thoughts. *It seems that playing by their rules doesn't work either. Look at Scarlett.* I thought about that as I made my way up the back staircase. As I reached the landing and was about to open the door, it opened inward to the stairwell.

"Oh, excuse me," I said, not recognizing the gentleman staring at me. Based on his clothing, he was a member.

"Excuse me," he said with a grin and a tip of his head.

The way his eyes scanned over me made my stomach twist, not in a good way.

I took a step to the right and one to the left. We seemed to be in a choreographed dance that had me blocked. I stepped backward, still holding the door. "You do realize the members have a separate staircase." I feigned a smile. "One much nicer than this."

His gaze lingered on my name tag for too long, before looking up and replying. "I'm on my way to the drivers' station."

"Oh," I said, realizing this man wasn't a member, but a driver.

The station he referred to was a separate building where the drivers could wait and pass time until they received a call. Knowing it was only almost four, I had a wash of pity that this man could be waiting there for hours.

"Please," he said, making room for me. "Ladies first, Rae."

"Thank you." My skin prickled as I passed. It was the unwelcome sensation that came with the combination of his unwanted stare and the way he said my name.

Once I was free and beyond his gaze, my body did a full-out shiver, and I smoothed my skirt. "Forget about him," I mumbled.

As I walked to the lounge, I thought about my earlier talk with Frankie. We'd only had a few minutes after my family left and before I needed to get ready for work. Now that he knew that I worked at the country club where he was a member, I found I was more open to talking about it. When I mentioned the Tertian Lounge, I could tell it made him uncomfortable.

"They're just a bunch of old men," I'd said. That was what I reminded myself as I stepped in the back door behind the bar.

Bette's bright smile met me as I entered. "Rae, some of the members have been asking for you."

"This is so odd."

"Most of them are out-of-towners, so enjoy the tips while you can."

"Most of them?" I asked, looking out at the large, plush room. I tried to recognize faces. The chairs were arranged in more intimate groupings, along with a few small tables, and some members were standing along the walls. The doors to the balcony were open, and more members were outside, surrounded by a fog of expensive cigar smoke.

Bette elbowed me and tilted her head. Sitting alone at a small table with one high-backed chair was a man I recognized, Henri Turner. "He's waiting."

Fastening the black apron over my skirt, I took the electronic tablet from where it was charging behind the bar. As I did, I peered out at the man waiting. Henri Turner wasn't a bad-looking man. Other than I assumed he was older than my mother, he had a distinguished air about him that Max Kluser and the man in the staircase definitely lacked. Maybe it was confidence that accompanied a net worth beyond my comprehension. Or maybe it was earned.

I heard he was high up in his family's company.

The first night I met him, Henri Turner had been a bit overwhelming. Now, I couldn't see him without remembering his mother and sister. A quick thought of my mother came to mind. I'd been lucky. Probably being raised by the venomous woman who believed the world should know she drank decaffeinated coffee could negatively affect a child's psyche.

en again, it seemed that Ashleigh Maxwell had turned out all right.

Psychology wasn't my field of study, but after working at the Cliffs, I decided it could be a good minor to accompany economics and business. After all, the men in this lounge shared the fruits of success, yet each one was different from the other.

"Rae," Mr. Turner said as he lifted his face from the screen of his phone. "I was beginning to wonder if you were scheduled." His lips curled. "I knew Bette wouldn't lead me astray."

"I'm here for the rest of the night, Mr. Turner. What can I get for you?"

CHAPTER

29

Bernie

With a huff, I entered my office and lifted the telephone from the cradle. "Fritz, tell me you didn't find someone else?"

"We didn't."

"Then, can this wait?"

"Probably," the sheriff said, "but I thought you might want to know some progress the medical examiner made."

"Is that progress going to help or hurt Woodland Cliffs?"

"I suppose that will depend."

Exhaling, I sat behind my desk, teetering on the edge of my chair with my elbows on the blotter. I had multiple notes scribbled here and there. I didn't live in the Stone Age. I knew how to make electronic notes and calendar entries. Sometimes, an old-fashioned pen or pencil scribbling thoughts helped a frantic mind.

Now, seeing what I'd written anew, I saw names that were better off not left as evidence. It was time for a new blotter.

The meeting the other day with the executive board had me thinking. I'd done a mental rundown on male members of the country club as well as male employees. I supposed it was sexist—a woman can kill women—but my gut said it was a man. My head didn't want there to be a connection to the club. It was my damn gut that wouldn't let that thought rest.

My problem was tying Ellen Temple to Scarlett Barrack or finding a common connection. No. My problem was time. I didn't have any, not this weekend.

"Fritz, I have a very busy club right now, and I'd prefer to be out and about, watching and listening."

"This is for your ears only."

"I'm listening," I said, leaning back in the chair as dusk fell beyond the windows.

"The coroner let it slip today that Miss Barrack was pregnant."

I sat forward. "Pregnant?"

My mind did the math. Scarlett went missing nearly six months ago.

When was the last time we...?

"How far along was she?"

"Only a few weeks," Fritz said as I stifled my sigh of relief. He went on. "She may not have even known."

"Or she did, and that's why she's dead."

"She didn't impregnate herself," Fritz said. "They're running the DNA."

I stood with the cordless telephone at my ear as I paced a trek near the windows. "Will you let me know?"

"Tell me that you're not worried it's yours."

My pacing stopped. "Hell no." If she'd been seven or eight months pregnant, that might have been an issue of concern. Yes, I'd screwed her. I had, but not in the last few weeks. "Tell me when you have a name and if there's a connection."

"Bernie, we talked after Ellen was found. You know as well as the rest of the world that there were problems in her paradise. We questioned people close to her who believed she was about to leave Henri Turner."

"He denies that."

"He does," Fritz said. "I keep thinking there's a connection to him, but how?"

"Scarlett worked here. She waited on him." I shook my head. "I've got nothing more."

"What about Max Kluser?" Fritz asked. "No one has pressed charges, but his name keeps popping up with some of your staff."

I clenched my teeth. My nostrils flared as I recalled walking in on Max the other night. His hands had been on his belt. Yes, he gave me a logical answer. His office had an attached bathroom. I'd surprised him. Yet I knew from some of the employees whom I bedded that

I wasn't alone in my affection for the staff. That bit of information was something neither of us wanted to be made public. "Up how?"

"It might be time for you to clean house, Bernie. Times are changing. If unacceptable behavior has been ignored..."

Shit.

"This isn't a good time."

"It never is. We're calling in some of your staff for follow-up questions."

"How long," I asked, "until the DNA comes back?"

"They put in a rush, but with the holiday, I'm not expecting miracles."

"Listen," I said, "I've known Max for years. I'll talk to him, but I just don't see him as a person who would take Scarlett, kidnap her" —I thought of the pictures Fritz showed me, the ones of the scars and the broken and healed bones— "and do God knows what. Just because a man likes a little on the side doesn't mean he's some sick fuck."

"It doesn't rule him out either."

"Thank you for letting me know," I said as the air filled with a loud boom and colors exploded across the sky, reflecting over the water.

"What was that?" Fritz asked.

"Fireworks. Tradition."

"Some traditions need to end. I'll call you if I learn more."

Hanging up the phone, I lingered near the window,

watching the colorful display. The more
about the chain of events, the more my thought
to Henri Turner. I picked up the phone and dialed a
number.

The recipient answered on the third ring.

"Mitchell," I said. "This is Bernie Maze."

"It's late, Bernie. What can I do for you?"

"I have a question for you?"

"All right."

I cleared my throat. "Did I hear you and Henri
Turner are working on a joint endeavor?"

"We've been putting together some models and
running numbers. Why?"

"How well do you know him?"

CHAPTER

30

Rae

I lifted my phone from the bedside stand and tried to focus on the screen. It was 9:15. That might sound late, but to someone who didn't crawl into bed until after two in the morning for the last four nights, nine was too early in the morning.

The notification that woke me was a text message from Frankie.

"Come out on your stoop. I have a surprise for you."

The part of me that desired more sleep wanted to groan and burrow into the covers. The part of me that hadn't seen Frankie since Thursday morning was smiling. A quick turn to my left and I saw Robyn, mostly her blond hair.

Quietly, I eased out of my bed. I made a quick stop at the bathroom, did my business, ran a toothbrush over my teeth, splashed my face with water, and combed my fingers through my hair before piling it on my head in a messy bun. In my sleeping shorts and a camisole, I walked barefoot down the hallway and into the living room. Keeping the chain lock engaged, I opened the door and peered out to the stoop.

The smile from earlier grew as I closed the door, unlocked the chain, and opened the door wider.

Frankie was standing with a cup of high-end coffee in his hand. "Two creams. One sugar."

"You remembered. Are you my surprise, or is it the coffee?"

"Both," he said, stepping forward and offering me a kiss. "I've missed seeing you."

"You could come to the club." I opened the door. "Do you want to come in?"

"This is a big step, Rae." His blue eyes sparkled in the sunshine. "Invite me in, and next, I'll be leaving a toothbrush."

"Whoa. You're moving a little fast." As Frankie followed me inside, I lowered my voice. "Robyn is here. She's asleep."

"Why is she here?" he asked.

I shrugged. "None of my business. I haven't pushed, but I can guess her summer plans with Parker didn't go the way she'd planned."

"Well, the bed will be crowded with all three of us, but I think I could manage."

Shaking my head, I led Frankie into the kitchen. "Do you want to share?" I lifted the cup.

"I was talking about sharing."

"No," I replied unequivocally. "I'm discussing coffee."

"I have a cup in the car. I thought maybe you'd want to go to breakfast with me."

I looked down at what I'd worn to bed. "I'm not dressed for public."

Frankie's cheeks rose in a smile. "I like the way you're dressed."

"I have food here. I had my family over for breakfast on Saturday. I could make us eggs, and I still have fruit."

"I forgot you said they were visiting. Are they still in town?"

"Yes, through Tuesday."

Frankie shook his head. "You've been busy. You don't need to cook for me."

"Do you know how to cook?"

"As a matter of fact, I do. Let me go get my coffee, and I'll be back."

Before I could protest, or say anything at all, Frankie was out the door and quickly back. With a grin, he walked past me into the kitchen and opened the refrigerator. Next, he started opening cupboards and the pantry.

"Make yourself at home," I said with a giggle as I curled one leg beneath me and sat at the kitchen table.

"Give me ten minutes," he said, "and you will have a Frankie special."

I waggled my eyebrows. "That sounds impressive." I tilted my head. "And fast."

Frankie walked to me and reached for my chin, lifting it until my lips met his. When he pulled away, I was met with an infectious grin. "Impressive, yes. And when *that* happens, speed will not be my goal."

"Sure of yourself."

He winked. "One step at a time, Rae. Let me see what you have here."

Robyn had bought groceries I didn't usually have. As Frankie removed fresh items from the refrigerator, I thought about stopping him, but that would mean not getting my Frankie special. Instead, I decided to sit back and watch. When I had the chance to shop, I'd replenish whatever he used.

I sat in awe as Frankie sliced and diced.

Feeling a bit unhelpful, I made more coffee.

Peppers and onions sizzled in a frying pan.

In no time, the kitchen smelled heavenly.

Once he had his special ready, Frankie set our plates on the table. "Ta-da." He tilted his head toward the flowers. "Those are nice. Did your mom and stepdad bring them?"

The vegetable omelet melted in my mouth as I took my first bite, and I grinned. Once I swallowed, I started with a compliment. "Oh my gosh, Frankie, this omelet is delicious. How did you learn to cook like this?"

"My mom."

"Thank you for the flowers. You know they're not

from my parents." It felt odd to refer to Mom and Eric in the plural form, but it was easier.

He sat down. "They're not. Who are they from?"

"I assumed you. I sent you a text saying thank you."

His expression turned quizzical. "I got the text, and I wasn't sure what you were thanking me for. I assumed it was for our time on the beach."

The omelet suddenly felt heavy in my stomach. "Are you serious, you didn't send the flowers?"

"I'd like to take credit, but no."

My skin cooled as I looked at the long-stemmed roses. All at once, I stood, gathered the roses together, and opening the cupboard to the trash, I threw them in the wastebasket. When I turned, Frankie's blue eyes were wide.

"What was that about?"

"I don't know," I said, shaking my head. "I thought roses were a bit much from you, but I figured you could afford..." I took a deep breath, telling myself not to be silly. I turned to Frankie's light-blue stare. "I don't know who they're from, and if you ask me, that's creepy."

"And they were addressed to you? Maybe Parker was sending an apology bouquet."

"No, they were for Rae," Robyn said, standing in the doorway. "Hi, Frankie."

"Hey." He stood up. "Do you want an omelet? I can make you one."

She shook her head. "No. I'll pass, but I do smell

coffee."

At nearly noon, I walked Frankie to the door. "Thank you for coming by." My cheeks rose as a smile grew. "It was sweet, and oh my, the omelets were fantastic."

"There are some advantages to still living at home —Mom's cooking."

"You don't have a chef or something?"

He reached for my hands. "I'd love to have you come to dinner one night and meet my parents."

I looked down and back up. "I met them at the club."

"You did?"

"Well, they only know I was their server. I didn't exactly say, here's your glass of wine, Mrs. Hamilton, and I think I like your son."

Frankie grinned. "You *think* you like me?"

"Maybe a little."

He leaned closer with more ease than the other day and brought his lips to mine. When the kiss ended, he said, "I think I like you too." He reached for my hand. "Do you work tonight?"

"Yes. It's the last shift for a while. I'll be off until Thursday." I remembered my family. "I did promise my mom and sister to spend tomorrow with them before they leave."

"I'm back to work on Tuesday, but make sure Tuesday evening and Wednesday are reserved for me."

"Deal."

CHAPTER

31

Rae

"Hey," Beth said, coming up behind me. I spun around as I took in my friend's smiling face. "Are you up here tonight?" Here being the Tertian Lounge.

"Yeah," she said with a shrug. "Half the out-of-town members have left, but we're still busy."

I reached for her hand. "I'm so glad you're here too." I wanted to ask who sent her and if she did anything to get this assignment, but I didn't. Maybe I didn't want to know the truth, or perhaps I didn't want her to lose her smile.

"Rae, Henri's back," Bette whispered.

Beth and I turned to see Mr. Turner sitting at the same table where he'd been for the last four nights.

"I'm so ready for a night off," I said as I collected the bottle of Black Label bourbon and a tumbler.

Mr. Turner's eyes were on me from the moment I

stepped around the bar. "Rae, what a pleasant surprise."

His voice was smooth, like syrup. It undoubtedly helped him in whatever he did professionally, but I found it unnerving, as if he were covering something more sinister with a sugary distraction.

"Mr. Turner, it's nice to see you."

"Will you be working tomorrow, too?"

"No, thank goodness."

"Don't tell me that you're unhappy here at the Cliffs."

"Not exactly unhappy," I said, "just ready for a break."

The same as he'd done the last four nights, Mr. Turner laid a hundred-dollar bill on the table. "For your bother."

"No bother," I said as I pushed the bill into the pocket of the apron.

When I got back to the bar, Beth's expression had changed. "I swear, he's a creep."

I nodded. "No argument here, but he tips well."

"That's what Scarlett said."

"What?"

"Nothing, it's just something I remembered."

"Well, stop," I said. "You just made him even creepier."

"Is that possible?" Beth asked, her grin back in place.

Unlike the previous nights, at near nine, another

man joined Mr. Turner. It didn't take a sixth sense to see that their discussion was tense.

"Should I go over there to take his order?" I asked Bette about the man with Mr. Turner.

Her lips formed a straight line as she nodded. "In and out."

"Who is the other guy?"

"That's Harrison Turner, Henri's older brother. You'll get used to seeing both of them. Let's just say, there's no love lost between those two."

As I approached, Harrison was leaning forward, and his voice was low, reminding me of a growl such as a dog's warning. "Ellen told Marley."

It was all I heard before they noticed me. "Hello, Mr. Turner, may I get you anything?"

"No, Rae," Henri Turner said, "he's leaving." His stare went back to his brother. "We can talk about your farfetched ideas in private, brother."

Harrison Turner turned to me. "Rae, is it? Yes, my brother is mistaken, as he often is. I'll have two fingers of Pappy, neat." He looked at his brother and back to me. "Oh, and have Bette put this on Henri's tab."

"You're delusional," Henri Turner said as I walked away.

"Two fingers of Pappy, neat," I said to Bette.

"Ten bucks says one of them throws a punch."

"Are they really that bad?"

"Always have been," she said. "I don't know when it started, but man, they are like oil and water."

As she handed me the drink, I said, "I met their sister, Ashleigh Maxwell. She seemed nice."

"Probably the best of the bunch, if you ask me." Bette lowered her voice. "Mom is a treat."

"Oh, I had the pleasure."

"So sorry," she called as I walked back to the men's table. My presence stilled whatever conversation they were having. I felt the small hairs on my arms come to attention as I neared. There was that much electricity crackling around them as if a storm were brewing. After placing a square napkin, I set the tumbler upon the table. "Please let me know if I can get either of you anything else."

Beth was right that this final night of the weekend was the least attended. By the time the fireworks exploded over the ocean, the lounge was nearly empty. At some point, the eldest Turner left—no punches thrown—leaving his brother alone with the bottle. A quick glance at the remaining bourbon and I knew Henri Turner had drunk more than any other night.

"Mr. Turner," I asked, "are you all right?"

"No, but things will take a turn soon."

"Do you need us to call your driver?"

He shook his head before a slow grin curled his lips. "Rae, you can drive me home."

His comment wasn't what I was expecting; nonetheless, I kept my server smile in place. "I believe that's against club rules. I don't mind calling someone else for you."

Henri Turner laid a second hundred-dollar bill on the table. "Thank you for the service, Rae." His hand was still on the bill. "I would be even more generous with a ride. My home isn't far."

"I'm sure you would." His creep factor was growing exponentially with each word of this conversation. It wasn't only what he said, but how he said it, how his eyes narrowed as he unashamedly stared at my breasts and slowly back to my eyes. "Please let me know if you want me to call."

"I'll drive myself." He lifted his hand off the bill. "Don't worry. I've had more to drink and made it home just fine."

Nodding, I went back to the bar to Bette and Beth. "I'm worried about him driving."

"Richard Reynolds is probably out in the lot waiting," Bette said.

"Who's Richard Reynolds?"

"He works for Henri." Bette shrugged. "He was up here the other day, but I think it was before you clocked in."

"Would he have taken the employee stairs?" I asked, recalling the odd encounter.

"Probably."

"Tall guy, short hair, weird?"

"You just described half the members and their drivers," Beth said, reaching into her apron and pulling out her tips. She looked up and smiled. "Better than downstairs even on a slower night."

Mr. Turner stood and nodded our direction. "Have a nice night, girls."

"You too," Bette said.

"Girls," I repeated under my breath with disgust.

"Good with the bad," Bette said as she looked over at Beth's tips.

CHAPTER

32

Rae

"**A**re you sure I look okay?" I asked Frankie as I smoothed the skirt of my sundress and adjusted the matching yellow cardigan.

"Stop worrying. I met your mom today, and I wasn't even planning on it."

I settled against the passenger seat in Frankie's work car and looked out at my Honda next to Robyn's car. I'd need to tell my apartment complex if Robyn was going to stay. Pretty soon someone would complain about the extra car.

"Earth to Rae."

Turning to Frankie, I smiled. "Sorry. It's just been a busy weekend, and I'm glad you got to meet my mom and Eric."

"I didn't know he was a policeman."

"He likes to tell people that. I feel sorry for Jendy when she's older. He'll probably wear his uniform to answer the door." I shook my head and looked out the window as Frankie began driving. "As a detective, Eric doesn't wear a uniform very often, but he was the first time Mom met him. I think that was the first step in what they have today."

"Ah, your mom likes a man in uniform?"

I nodded.

"What about you?"

I scanned Frankie from his light-brown hair, down his button-down shirt, his sleeves rolled up to his elbows, and his khaki shorts and leather loafers. "You look nice when you dress for work."

"You're saying that I don't look nice now?"

"You do." I reached out to his arm. "This is the you I'm used to." I was. It was how he dressed for classes most of the time. "I'm a little disappointed you didn't pick me up on the motorcycle."

Frankie grinned. "My parents would not approve. And besides, you look too pretty in that dress to be on the back of a bike."

"I'm getting used to it."

"Good," he said.

My expression dimmed. "Speaking of your parents, what should I tell them that I do?"

"My mom knows. I told her that you said you waited on them." He grinned. "She said she remembered you."

My stomach twisted. "Is that good or bad?"

"It depends." He tilted his head and grinned.

"Were you the one who spilled the wine on her new white blouse?"

"What? No!"

Frankie laid his hand on my knee. "I'm joking. It's good. Why are you so nervous?"

"Because working at the Cliffs makes me think that there are two sets of people, and we're not in the same set."

"Not all the people who belong to the Cliffs are stuck-up, arrogant assholes."

"Some are."

Frankie laughed. "You're right."

The scenery changed as Frankie drove us higher into the hills. It seemed like we were above the clouds when Frankie pushed a button beside a gate. The large iron fencing moved quietly to one side, allowing us entry. My eyes widened as I took in the Hamiltons' home. With each passing minute, I was certain this was a mistake. I didn't belong here.

When Frankie opened my door and offered me his hand, I felt a bit lighter. "Are you sure?" I asked.

"Come on, Rae. My parents don't bite."

With my hand in his, Frankie escorted me up the steps, and the door opened. I recognized his mom from the Cliffs, but this time, she was wearing a simple top and blue jeans. Her smile was contagious as she opened her arms and offered me a hug.

"Rae, it's good to finally formally meet you."

"Mrs. Hamilton."

"Oh, stop. I'm Audrey, and Frankie's father is Mitch. I'm so glad you could join us. Come on in." I peered over my shoulder, smiling at Frankie as his mom led us through a beautiful living room and toward the back of the house to a kitchen that looked as if it had been plucked from the page of a decorating magazine.

"This is lovely." I inhaled. "And something smells delicious."

"I hope you like lasagna. I made it without meat. I wasn't sure."

"I do. Lasagna sounds amazing, but yes, I would eat meat too."

"Is this Rae?"

We all turned to Mr. Hamilton's entrance and boisterous greeting.

"Yes, Dad," Frankie said, "this is Rae."

"Well, you should have told us that you were *the* Rae when we were at the Cliffs."

The Rae.

Warmth filled my cheeks.

"You are as pretty as Frankie said."

I looked at Frankie. "You really told them about me?"

"Only for the last year, Rae," Audrey said with a grin. "I'm so glad he finally asked you out."

"And you said yes," his father added.

I was a bit taken aback—in a good way—at the light and easy atmosphere. As Audrey removed the lasagna from the oven and a salad bowl from the refrigerator, I offered to help.

"Nonsense. Today, you relax and we'll serve you."

It wasn't until we left, walking to Frankie's car, that he finally reached for my hand and gave it a squeeze. "See, they weren't scary."

"They really weren't. It's crazy how different people are. I was wrong to lump all the members in one group." I looked up at the stars. "It was also nice to spend time without talking about Scarlett."

"It's a sad situation, but you're not her. No lumping."

"I like that. No lumping."

He opened my door, and once I was seated, he closed it and came around to the other side. "You must be tired, Rae, but how about a walk on the beach?"

"Garrapata."

He nodded.

"I'd like that."

The stars twinkled as we drove along Highway 1.

After Frankie pulled the car over to the gravel, he came around and opened my door. Yes, I could open my own door, but having him do it, and reach for my hand, felt...special.

We held hands as we slowly descended the wooden stairs. As our feet found the sand, Frankie pulled me closer and kissed me. "My mom wasn't lying, Rae. I've been talking about you since the first time we met. There was something about you. I felt on edge, like I couldn't talk to you, but I wanted to be with you. It was a different feeling. I tried to ignore it, but then you'd smile at something I'd say, or you'd wow us all with your understanding of whatever was being taught." He shook his head. "I'm saying this all wrong."

"No, Frankie, you're saying it just right."

"Tomorrow night, how about a picnic here?"

"It's a date."

CHAPTER

33

Rae

As he'd done on our first kind-of date, Frankie picked me up on his motorcycle. When he came to the door dressed in jeans, I knew he had. My smile grew at the sight of him. What I'd told him last night was accurate. I liked the way he dressed for work and the more casual man I'd met at school. Scanning him from his hair to his shining blue orbs, down his wide shoulders, toned torso, and long legs, I liked this Frankie too.

His grin met mine. "You're wearing jeans and boots."

"I was hoping for the bike."

Taking a step forward, he softly kissed me in the doorway. "Your chariot awaits."

"Come in while I get my purse, and I have a surprise."

Frankie's eyebrows danced. "I like surprises." His gaze soon met my new roommate's. "Hi, Robyn."

"Sorry to be a third wheel."

"I'd offer to have you join us," Frankie said, "but I don't think we'll all fit on my bike."

"Are you kidding? Rae's been excited about the bike all day. I wouldn't think of barging in."

"Another night," he said.

With a small purse to hold my phone, I pulled a white box from the refrigerator.

"What's that?" Frankie asked.

"It's the surprise."

He smirked. "Not what I was hoping for."

"You don't know what's in there."

"All I want is you."

"Go," Robyn said, waving her hand. "I'm getting a cavity."

"We won't be too late," I said as Frankie opened the door. When I saw the way he was looking at me, something inside twisted. "Or maybe we will."

Robyn's laugh faded as we closed the door.

"Will this fit in the saddlebag?" I asked.

"Has she told you what happened?"

I shook my head as we walked to Frankie's bike. "I haven't asked. I don't want to pry. Since she started back at the day care, she's been better."

"Parker seemed..." Frankie shook his head. "I know he liked Robyn. I can't imagine him breaking it off like this." He took the box and lifted it, giving it a slight shake.

"Stop, you'll mess it up."

"Bakery box. Smells sweet. Something with frosting?"

"You have to wait," I said, after the box was secure and we put on our helmets.

Frankie got on his bike first, and soon, I was behind him, my arms around his torso.

The helmets weren't the fancy kind with microphones. So, instead of talking, I leaned against his back and watched as the Monterey countryside sped by in a blur. The sun was on its way down as we cruised along Highway 1.

Frankie carried the other bags as I carried the box down the wooden steps.

When we reached the bottom, I turned in all directions. "It's odd that a place this beautiful is always empty."

"It's because this is our place, Rae."

We settled on the blanket, both taking off our boots and socks. I rolled the hem of my jeans as Frankie opened the bottle of wine. After pouring me a glass, he handed it my way. "Thank you for going to my house. I may be lame, but I like my parents."

"It's not lame. I think this last weekend, I realized, I like mine too. It's weird to think of Eric as my parent, but he's great with Jendy and he makes Mom happy." I twisted the stem, watching the rose-colored liquid swirl. When I looked up, I added, "Your parents are good people. You should like them." Warmth filled my cheeks. "I can't believe you told them about me."

Lying back on the blanket, Frankie held his head with his elbow on the ground. "My mom is..." He shrugged. "Easy to talk to. Before she got involved in the winery and vineyards, she was a counselor. I think she used that psychology stuff on her kids. Susan, my older sister, and I have always been able to talk about anything."

Sitting with my legs crisscrossed, I turned until we were facing each other. "Remember what you said about lumping?"

Frankie nodded as he set his glass in the sand.

"We all do it. When we're younger, we lump our parents into a group that includes everyone's. When my dad got sick—" I took a deep breath.

Frankie sat up as his hand came to my knee. "Don't talk about something you don't want to."

I shook my head. "I want to. If you don't mind hearing it."

Standing, he brushed the sand from his jeans and offered me his hand. Setting my glass in the soft sand, I put my palm in his.

"The sun is about to set," Frankie said. "Let's walk on the beach."

With my hand in his, I looked at our picnic. "I guess there's no one here to take our food."

"Bears stay inland."

I shook my head. "You're kidding."

With our feet bare, we walked toward the sea. The sun glistened, turning the horizon shades of orange and red as it shone like diamonds upon the water.

"When he got sick, my attitude changed. You know, you always think you have forever. When I realized I didn't, I stopped being a teenager. I grew up, faster than some. I had to fit fifty years with my dad into seventeen. I'd been standoffish, and I had too little time to make up for that."

Frankie stopped walking and reached for my other hand. Holding them both, he smiled down at me. The sky's colors reflected in his light-blue stare. "You loved him."

It wasn't a question, but I nodded, holding back the tears.

The thing was, I hadn't talked to anyone about this in years. Robyn was my freshman roommate, and everything was too raw. She knew the story but not this. Beth knew parts too. These were feelings I'd kept to myself.

He squeezed my hands. "I bet he knew."

"I hope he did. I also think that seeing Mom and Eric last weekend reminded me that I need to be better with Mom. I lost one parent, I want to keep both her and Eric."

Letting go of my hands, Frankie palmed my cheeks and held my gaze to his. "I don't think I like you, Rae." Before I could respond, his voice grew husky. "I know I do. I care about my parents, but like I said, I want to live my own life. The good news is that they both loved you. Mom couldn't wait to talk to me after I took you home."

My eyes closed, and when they opened, he was still there, holding my face. "I liked them too."

"I'd like to give us time."

I nodded.

"I'm not sure what I'm supposed to ask, but I'd like us to be exclusive."

A smile lifted my cheeks. "Me too."

As his lips met mine, I leaned against him. My breasts flattened against his chest as he wrapped his arms around me and pulled me even closer. For a moment, a magical moment, there was only us. With a fiery sunset and waves lapping our feet, the world felt right.

The sky darkened as we made our way to our picnic.

"Tell me my surprise," he said as we both sat and lifted our glasses of wine.

"A large slice of red velvet cake with cream cheese frosting."

Frankie's hand went to his chest. "My favorite. How did you know?"

"Would you believe that I've seen you eat it at the campus bakery?"

"You were watching me?"

Warmth filled my cheeks. "Yes."

CHAPTER

34

Rae

"I had a great time," I said as Frankie walked me toward my apartment door after our picnic. My statement wasn't untrue. Being with him did something to me in a new way, a way I hadn't felt—well, ever. We weren't kids, as I'd been in high school. Life was different.

Did that mean I thought of Frankie as my forever?

I couldn't answer that. I could say, I liked that he was my now.

"Do you want to come in?" I asked.

"As long as Robyn doesn't mind."

"She's good."

The apartment was darker than I expected as I unlocked the door and pushed it inward. "She must be asleep already."

Frankie looked at his watch. "It's not even eleven."

I lifted my finger to my lips as I turned on a light. "I'll go close the bedroom door."

As I walked quietly down the hallway, my thoughts were on the beach, the wine, the food, and Frankie. While I felt like we were taking things slow, I also felt that each move either of us made was monumental. It was as if we both wanted to move forward but were both too timid to do so.

I reached for the door handle. The light from the hallway spilled over the floor and bed. The covers were moved, but the bed was empty. "Robyn?" I called, walking into the bedroom.

After checking the bathroom and closet, I came back down the hall. "Robyn?"

Frankie stepped from the kitchen with a water bottle. "Isn't she in bed?"

"No," I said, my lips pursing. "It's weird." I went to the front door and opened it. Her Chevy was exactly where it had been. "My car is gone."

"What?" Frankie asked. "Why would she take your car?"

I hurried back down the hallway and opened the drawer I knew Robyn used for her purse. "Her purse is here."

"Does she use your car often?"

"No. Never. Well, never until now."

"Why don't you try to call her?"

Nodding, I retrieved my phone from my purse and hit her number. I heard three rings and her voice mail.

I tried it again. Same result. My gaze met Frankie's. "This is weird."

"You have work tomorrow. Do you have keys to her car? I can pick you up."

"I don't have to be there until three. You'll be at the winery." I hurried back to the bedroom and looked in Robyn's purse. As I did, I felt a bit like I was invading her privacy, but then again, if she took my car... "I found her keys," I said, holding up the fob.

"Where were your keys?"

"Hanging on a hook in the kitchen. Maybe she just had to run out for something." I pulled back a flap on her purse. "Her phone is here."

"That's strange."

I wrapped my arms around my own midsection as I shook my head. "This isn't like Robyn. I know she's going through something, but she doesn't just disappear. And why take my car?"

Frankie pulled his phone from the pocket of his blue jeans. "Do you have Parker's number?"

"I bet it's on Robyn's phone."

A few minutes later, I disconnected the call. "You're right. He didn't break up with her. He hasn't heard from her since she left. He says he's left messages, but she hasn't returned them."

"Did he say what happened between them?"

I shook my head. "Only that he doesn't know why she left."

"I'll stay with you."

"Frankie..."

He took ahold of my hand. "Not like that, Rae. I like Robyn, and you're upset. I'll just hang out, and once she's here, I'll go home."

Frankie was right; I was upset. It didn't make sense, none of it.

"You could call the police," Frankie said as we turned on an old movie I'd seen probably twenty-five times. "And report a missing person."

"Can I?" I asked. "Don't they have to be missing longer?"

"A car is missing too. You could call that in."

I leaned back against the couch next to Frankie, thinking how ridiculous it was that I could report a car before a person. "I don't want to get her in trouble. I'm sure there's a logical explanation."

My thoughts were on Robyn as the movie started.

When my eyes opened, Frankie and I were a tangled mess on the living room floor and the sun was streaming through the patio doors. "Shit."

He woke with a start, lifting himself to sitting. "I told you that movie was boring."

The excitement of waking next to him was immediately overcome by worry. "Still no Robyn."

Frankie ran his hand over his face and stood. "Do you mind if I make some coffee?"

"Please. I need to do a few things."

He grinned. "Me too. I'll make the coffee first."

As I walked down the hall, questions swirled in my

thoughts. I couldn't make sense of what was happening. Robyn had walked out on Parker with no excuse. Would she do the same to me?

I didn't think so.

I didn't think she would. She also wouldn't walk out with my car.

It was as I came out of the bathroom that I saw the alarm on Frankie's face.

"What is it?"

He looked up from his phone. "There was a break in the Scarlett Barrack case. My dad said to meet him at the office. He said you should come too."

"How does your dad know about it?"

"Apparently, the executive board of the Cliffs was notified."

"What does that mean?"

"I don't know," Frankie admitted.

My phone rang. The screen read Woodland Sheriff Department.

I turned the screen toward Frankie, letting him read the words, before answering.

"Hello," I said with a bit of trepidation.

"Is this Rae Watson?"

"Yes, I'm Rae."

"Miss Watson, we need you to come down to the station."

My hands began to tremble. "I-I don't have my car."

"We can send an officer to your address."

I covered the phone. "They want me to come to the station. Will you drive me?"

"Yes," he said. "I'll text my dad."

"I have a friend who can bring me. Is everything all right?"

"Please hurry."

"Maybe you should call Eric?" Frankie recommended as we left my apartment.

"And say what?"

Frankie shook his head. "I don't know, but my dad is meeting us at the station."

"I don't understand what's happening."

I looked down as my phone began to vibrate. I had missed calls from Beth and one from Chad. My phone vibrated again. It was McKenzie.

"What's going on?" Frankie asked.

"Three calls in a row from people at work."

"Should you call them back?"

"If they want me to come in early, I can't say, oh, after the sheriff's department."

The city of Woodland was coming to life as the day began. People walked the sidewalks, going in and out of cafés, and cars moved along the roads as if there weren't some looming storm cloud about to rain down. My stomach growled as we pulled into the sheriff's station parking lot.

For as early as it was, I was a bit surprised to see people gathered near the door. One woman stepped in front of me. "Miss, are you here about the kidnapping?"

Frankie reached for my hand and tugged me toward the doors before I could compute the question.

Kidnapping.

We stopped at the front desk and spoke to a woman in uniform. "Hello, I'm Rae Watson. I got a call—"

She interrupted me as she stood. "Please come with me."

I looked at Frankie and back to the officer. "May my friend come too?"

"No, I'm sorry. He'll need to wait out here."

"Excuse me." A louder voice came from the entry. I turned to see Mr. Hamilton. He wasn't alone. There was a smartly dressed woman at his side, one I didn't recognize. "Officer, this is Ruth Hamersley."

I'd heard that name.

Was it at the country club?

I couldn't think.

Mr. Hamilton continued, "Ms. Hamersly is Miss Watson's attorney."

"My attorney?"

"You can't question my client," Ms. Hamersley said, stepping forward, "without representation."

The officer lifted her hands. "Miss Watson isn't being questioned."

"I-I still want her with me," I said, more than

willing to accept the help Mr. Hamilton thought I needed.

Nervously, I looked at my new attorney as we followed the officer. Up until that moment, I hadn't considered why I was here. And as the officer opened the door, I was completely unprepared for what I saw.

Wrapped in a blanket with her hair a mess, bruises on her face, and bandages on her wrists and ankles, was my friend.

"Oh my God, Robyn," I said as I rushed toward her.

"Rae." Tears streamed down her cheeks. "He thought I was you. He kept calling me Rae."

"Who?"

CHAPTER

35

Rae

Three months later- Labor Day weekend

"How are classes, Rae?" Audrey asked as I helped her carry bowls of food to the outdoor table.

Their backyard was beautiful, with the pool glistening in the sunlight, the tables set up, and the ocean for the perfect backdrop.

"They just started, but you know, they're classes," I said with a smile. "I'm excited for this to be my last year."

"So is Frankie."

I nodded. I knew what Frankie was thinking. Since early June, we'd become closer. As a matter of fact, he was now living with me, toothbrush and all.

"Do you really have this picnic every year?" I asked.

"I like to entertain."

"There's so much food."

Her blue eyes shimmered. "Well, I have a secret, if you promise not to tell."

"I love secrets... Well, I used to."

"This one is benign," she whispered. "While you know I love to cook, I didn't make this food. I had it catered."

"I'll never tell."

In the last three months, I'd gotten to know Frankie's parents better, and with each encounter—including Frankie's announcement about an address change—I liked them more. Audrey was truly a beautiful woman, inside and out. Not only was she a wonderful cook and mother to Frankie and his older sister, she went the extra mile for everyone.

It was just natural for her.

Frankie's sister Susan was here for the party. She normally resided in Napa. Three years older than Frankie, she'd already made her move in the world of the Hamilton Winery and Vineyard.

Audrey had stepped in as a friend and retired counselor after the kidnapping. She'd even invited Robyn to stay at their house. Although Audrey no longer practiced as a licensed therapist, she managed to give Robyn a safe environment, one where Robyn could work beyond the edge of her experience.

That's what Audrey called it—*the edge*.

According to her, the edge was the precipice where

a person must make a decision—step back or go over. It wasn't that every cliff was like the ones on the seaside near Woodland. The way she described it, the edge was meant to be breached. That's what Audrey helped Robyn do, to move forward.

She helped me too.

I felt guilty, knowing I'd been the target.

Robyn's and my ongoing joke about being twins had definitely lost its humor.

A man named Richard Reynolds was arrested for the murder of Scarlett Barrack. His case still hadn't gone to trial; there were big-league attorneys involved. It was that break in Scarlett's case that had saved Robyn. After she'd been pulled from my bed in my apartment and the car had been taken— the police believed the car was taken to create the ruse that I'd left town—Richard took Robyn to his home.

Technically, the house belonged to Henri Turner.

When the sheriff's deputies had arrived at the residence to bring Richard in for questioning in Scarlett's case, they also had a warrant allowing them to search the premises. What they found was like some sick crime show. Richard had chained Robyn to a large bolt in a suite farthest away from the rest of the house. That was why her ankles were so bruised.

According to reports, no one else in the household was aware of Richard's activities. It happened that his undoing was a small bit of evidence he'd unintentionally left with Scarlett before he killed her—the baby she carried had Richard's DNA.

"Audrey, is there anything else I can do to help?" Robyn asked.

"No, Robyn, please rest."

"I'm fine."

"I can help too," Parker said as he came up behind Robyn, wrapping his arm around her waist. "You should listen to Mrs. Hamilton," he whispered as he laid his hand over her baby bump.

Unlike Scarlett's ordeal, this baby was growing stronger by the day. Learning she was pregnant was why Robyn ran from Long Beach. Once Parker was told what had happened and about the baby, he was at Robyn's side. Looking at the two of them made me grin.

Frankie stepped forward and tugged my hand until he brushed a kiss over my lips. "You're not a server, Rae. You can relax too."

I wasn't a server.

After what happened to Robyn, I gave my notice, effective immediately, and I hadn't stepped foot back in the Cliffs. I'd taken Robyn's advice and agreed to a part-time job at the day care. I'd saved most of my tip money, and with my new roommate, I was set for the rest of this year.

Mrs. Maxwell had contacted me a few weeks ago and asked about my degree. Business and economics from Cal State had her attention. She confided that the executive board was interested in making some significant changes and proposed I should call her in the early spring. She said that during our brief discussion, she had seen the type of executive who could help to modernize Woodland Cliffs. While Bernie Maze was still the CFO, Max Kluser was no longer employed.

I didn't think I'd take her offer, but the idea of being an effective part of positive change was appealing. There was also the prospect of a job with Hamilton Winery in my future. I wasn't ready to make that decision. The biggest obstacle was Mitch's new partner.

Speaking of whom, he was walking our direction, with his new girlfriend on his arm. After Richard was arrested, Henri Turner's life took a turn, or as Audrey would say, jumped off the edge. He sold his home, agreed to an equitable split regarding his stake in Turner Industries, met a new woman, and announced his partnership with Hamilton Winery.

"Rae, it's nice to see you," Henri Turner said with a nod.

"Mr. Turner."

After a moment of polite conversation, Frankie took my hand and led me toward the house. "You don't like him, do you?"

"He has a vibe."

"It's because of all he's been through. It's sad people think the worst. Dad said Henri was as broken up as anyone to learn what had been happening in his home."

"I don't understand how they ruled him out."

Frankie shrugged as we entered the kitchen. His voice was low. "Reynolds confessed. Reynolds was also the one who impregnated Scarlett."

"And they couldn't have both been in on it?"

"And you tell Robyn she watches too many crime shows."

"I prefer the podcasts."

Backing me toward a counter, Frankie held on to the edge, caging me between his strong arms. "The salt water degraded the evidence except for the baby. Reynolds also ordered the furniture for the room, and members of the staff recalled him taking food. They just never questioned it."

"The furniture was for me," I said with my stomach twisting.

He leaned closer, his body as my shield. His voice declared my safety as he had since Robyn had been taken. "Reynolds is in jail, Rae. The evidence all pointed to him. You and Robyn are safe." He looked out to the yard. "Mom said she hopes it works out for Sarah and Henri. Mom thinks Sarah will be good for Henri. Hopefully, she'll help him move on, too."

"If you ask me, Sarah should be scared."

"Henri isn't like that. If anything, he lacks emotion. I've known him for a long time."

Lacks emotion.

Hadn't I heard that about serial killers?

Maybe I was listening to too many podcasts.

217

Back out on the deck, I stopped with my hand in Frankie's and watched as guests mingled about. Concentrating on life's positives, I took in the stunning view, my gaze going out to the ocean and back. Once again, I was in awe that I was a guest here in the Hamiltons' home, welcomed and loved. "Remember when you said that not all members of the Cliffs are assholes?"

Frankie's grin shone my direction. "I think I said *arrogant* assholes, but yes."

"Henri Turner is one. You know him as an equal. He has a power-trip thing. I waited on him enough at the Cliffs that I can say that with certainty. I don't know what Sarah sees in him." I shrugged. "Maybe kids. They're not getting younger."

"Not kids," Frankie said as we stepped back down onto the green carpet of grass.

"How would you know that?"

"I heard Mom and Dad talking. Henri Turner can't have kids, something about scarlet fever as a child."

Scarlett?

A shiver ran down my spine.

CHAPTER

36

Rae

Six Weeks Later

"I can't believe I'm back here," I said, looking around the dining room at the Cliffs.

Frankie's hand snaked around my waist pulling me to his side. "You're a guest, now."

I was.

After deciding to accept the Hamilton's invitation to attend this year's Harvest Gathering at Woodland Cliffs, Audrey insisted that I join her shopping. That afternoon trip resulted in the dress and shoes I'm now wearing. While they were much more comfortable than the ones the servers wore, they were equally as high.

"Is Henri Turner going to be here?" I asked in a whisper as a hostess I didn't recognize led us to our table.

Frankie's lips smiled, but his blue eyes were filled with concern. That emotion was for me, because he knew the way I felt about his father's new business partner.

"He isn't. Dad said that he and Sarah are out on their boat."

Boat.

Henri and Sarah Turner recently married, and their boat was really a yacht. A crew and the whole nine yards.

He won't be here.

I let out a breath as the weight of a possible encounter lifted from my shoulders.

"Relax." Frankie kissed my cheek before pulling out a chair for me.

After we were all seated, the hostess informed us that Beth would be our server.

My brow furrowed as I turned to Frankie. "Beth? She sent me a text saying she was moving away."

"Maybe it's another Beth."

"Rae," Audrey said, changing my focus. "We're so happy you agreed to join us. The Harvest Gathering is one of the biggest events here at the Cliffs."

"When Frankie was young, he was all about the pumpkin carving contest," Mitch said.

"I won it two years in a row," Frankie said with a grin.

"Two years?" I said with a grin. "How have you kept this secret from me?"

Audrey leaned forward. "Come talk to me any time. I will fill you in on everything. I even have pictures."

"And home movies," Frankie added. "I recommend you avoid the hours of my choir performances."

"Mr. and Mrs. Hamilton—" Beth said seconds before her eyes met mine. "Rae."

"I thought you moved away."

"I did. But I'm back." She shook her head. "I'm sorry. I'm Beth," she said to the entire table. "I'm here to serve you tonight. May we start with drinks?"

There was something about my friend that felt— off. As I watched her talking, I saw that she had lost weight and her complexion was paler than before.

Where had she gone?

"Rae, would you like a drink?"

Her use of my name pulled me from my thoughts. "A glass of chardonnay. Call me."

With a smile, Beth nodded and walked away.

"You two know one another?" Audrey asked.

"She is my friend who got me the job here. We met at community college and both switched to Cal State. But then right after classes began, Beth said she was moving." I shrugged. "She text that she was moving. It was weird."

Audrey's expression was puzzled. "She must have changed her mind."

"I don't know what it is, but she seems different."

"Maybe it's weird to serve you, her friend," Frankie suggested.

"You're probably right."

As the night progressed, I saw more of the people I used to work beside. Chad came up to the table. I introduced him to Frankie. Even McKenzie stopped to say hi. Seeing them made me feel bad that when I'd walked away from the job, I'd also fallen out of touch with my co-workers and friends.

At one point, Mitch and Audrey went over to the Turner's table to congratulate Mrs. Turner on her new daughter-in-law. It was then that I noticed Mrs. Turner-Maxwell was obviously pregnant. Thinking about the nice offer to work here after I finish my degree and how friendly she'd been to me, I was happy she and her husband were expecting a child.

"May I bring you dessert?" Beth asked after our dinner dishes were taken away.

I shook my head. In all the time I worked here, I never ate the food, nothing more than a nibble. Our dinner was delicious. After Mitch told Beth we were done for the evening, he grinned at Frankie and me. "Would you like to have an after dinner drink out on the patio?" His smile grew. "I hear this year's pumpkins are spectacular." He lowered his voice. "They use patterns and stencils. Not like when you were the champion."

Frankie looked at me and tilted his head. "Would you like to see this year's carvings?"

Knowing that I wouldn't turn a corner and run into Henri Turner made it easier to accept. "How can I turn down the opportunity to be seen with a two-time pumpkin carving champion?"

The autumn breeze rustled the orange and white lights in the trees as the four of us made our way to the side patio. The line of carved pumpkins was unbelievable. The carvings were intricate and looked professionally done, not by members' children. Some pumpkins had faces while others were characters from Marvel and DC comics.

With a crackling flame in the table before us, the four of us settled on soft sofas.

"I've always loved this patio," Audrey said.

I leaned closer to Frankie as I looked around at the clusters of sofas and fire tables. "I've never been out here before."

"Really?" Frankie asked.

"Not on this patio. I only worked here for about a month. I was in the dining room and the Tertian Lounge."

Mitch shook his head. "See, if I'd known you were Frankie's Rae..."

I grinned at the handsome man with his arm around me, thinking how funny it was that I liked being referred to as Frankie's Rae.

"...as a board member, I would have advised against the Tertian Lounge."

"The tips were fantastic."

"Well, honey," Audrey said, "when you run this place, you can turn down the testosterone in that lounge."

I snickered. "I don't think I'll be running Woodland Cliffs."

"Ashleigh Maxwell has her eye on you," Mitch said. "That woman can be tenacious." He lowered his voice, "like her mother."

"Speaking of that family," Audrey said, "isn't that Sarah over there with Ashleigh?"

We all turned as the small hairs on my arms stood to attention.

It was Sarah, Sarah Turner. She seemed animated as her hands moved as she spoke.

"I thought you said they were out on their boat?" I questioned.

Frankie and I looked at Mitch, who shrugged. "I guess their plans changed." He pulled his phone from his pocket. "I'll give Henri a text and see if he's here."

I reached for Frankie's hand.

"Mom, Dad," Frankie said, "we need to head out."

"I know Henri makes you uncomfortable, Rae," Mitch said, "but working with him, he's got a great business mind and all he talks about is Sarah."

Frankie and I stood. "It's okay," Frankie said. "We'll see you on Sunday." He leaned down and offered his mom a kiss on her cheek. "Thanks for dinner."

After our goodbyes, Frankie and I walked toward

the parking lot. For a moment, I stopped and stared out at a path, one that was more overgrown than it had been my first night at the Cliffs.

"What are you thinking?" Frankie asked.

"See that path over there?"

"Yes."

"It leads down a very steep path to the beach. The workers used to go there after closing and unwind."

"Is that where Ellen Temple jumped?"

I shook my head. "No, because if it was, the people working in there" —I jutted my chin toward the club— "would have seen her. They didn't."

With my hand in Frankie's, we walked away from the path and toward his car.

On Sunday morning, I woke as Frankie wrapped his arms around me and pulled me close. Rolling until we were face to face, I grinned. "Good morning."

"Good morning."

My body melted against his as we kissed.

The bedroom filled with the sound of notifications coming from Frankie's phone. With a giggle, I backed away. "Someone wants to get ahold of you."

He shook his head. "I prefer to hold you."

"Okay, hold that thought. You can check your phone, and I'll be back in a minute."

Frankie let out a sigh. "Fine."

As I came back from the bathroom, Frankie was standing, with his phone at his ear.

"You don't know any more?" Frankie said as his

head shook. As he turned my way, his blue eyes were round and wide.

Sitting on the edge of the bed, I waited for him to stop talking. Once he did, I asked, "What's going on?"

"Henri never returned Dad's text."

I shrugged. "So?"

"Bernie Maze called Dad early this morning."

My pulse was increasing with each phrase. "About?"

Frankie shook his head. "They found Henri Turner's body, on the beach, south of the Cliffs."

I stood. "What? He's dead?"

Frankie nodded as his brow furrowed. "Sarah seemed upset last night on the patio."

My fingertips were at my lips as I paced back and forth. "After the Harvest Gathering. That was when Ellen Temple was found." I turned to Frankie. "She was engaged to Henri and now it's Henri."

"The board is having an emergency meeting."

"Isn't Mrs. Turner on the board?"

"Dad said he'd call after the meeting."

CHAPTER

37

Ashleigh Turner-Maxwell

One Month Later

"Thank you for meeting me here, Sarah."

My sister-in-law nodded. "I should not have come here that night."

"You were upset. It was right for you to come talk to us. You were worried."

Sarah looked around the dining room at the Cliffs and lowered her tone. "I can't believe he did it."

I leaned back as my son squirmed within me. "Sarah, I'm so sorry. I've been concerned about my brother forever. I always worried that he would do something. I never imagined he'd take his own life."

"The crew said he'd been drinking. I keep hoping it was an accident, that he simply fell overboard."

"Mrs. Maxwell, Mrs. Turner."

I turned to the pretty redhead. "Hello."

name is Beth. I'm here to serve you. Would you like a drink?"

I placed my hand over my enlarged midsection. "Lemonade."

"I'm glad you're back," Sarah said to Beth.

The server's lips curled into a smile. "I'm very glad to be back."

"Was your time away what you expected?"

"No, Mrs. Turner, but it all ended well." Her gaze met Sarah's. "I'm sorry to hear about your husband's accident."

Sarah sat taller. "Thank you, Beth. I'll have a glass of cabernet."

Beth nodded and stepped away.

"Do you know her?" I asked.

"Not really. We helped one another out, once." Sarah shook her head. "I'm glad you asked me here. Henri told me that the Cliffs wanted to create a scholarship for the employees in Scarlett Barrack's name."

"Yes, we talked about that."

"I would like to offer a portion of Henri's life insurance to start that scholarship."

"Sarah, you don't—"

"I'm not on the edge about this. I think it's the right thing to do." Sarah smiled. "Henri would want that."

Thank you for reading ON THE EDGE.

* * *

Have you read GRAVITY? Gravity is a short story and Aleatha's contribution to NIGHTINGALE, a limited-time anthology benefiting Ukraine. In GRAVITY prominent characters from Aleatha's worlds gather at Woodland Cliffs for a very special occasion. You're invited. Never fear, Rae Watson, the new director of services, is there to help.

If you enjoyed this new-adult romantic thriller, please check out Aleatha's Light duet, beginning with INTO THE LIGHT.

Her newest contemporary romance series, the Sin Series, is about to conclude. Jump in today with book one, RED SIN.

For all of Aleatha's titles, from romantic thrillers to mafia romance, to lighter ones and erotic romance, check out her website or turn to "Books By Aleatha" in the backmatter.

Stay informed by signing up to receive Aleatha's newsletter.

What to do now

LEND IT: Did you enjoy *ON THE EDGE?* Do you have a friend who'd enjoy *ON THE EDGE? ON THE EDGE* may be lent one time. Sharing is caring!

RECOMMEND IT: Do you have multiple friends who'd enjoy my romantic thriller? Tell them about ON THE EDGE! Call, text, post, tweet...your recommendation is the nicest gift you can give to an author!

REVIEW IT: Tell the world. Please go to the retailer where you purchased this book, as well as Goodreads, and write a review.

Please share your thoughts about *ON THE EDGE* on:

*Amazon, *ON THE EDGE* Customer Reviews

*Barnes & Noble, *ON THE EDGE,* Customer Reviews

*Apple Books, ON THE EDGE Customer Reviews

* BookBub, ON THE EDGE Customer Reviews

*Goodreads.com/Aleatha Romig

Books by ALEATHA

RECENTLY RELEASED:

STAND-ALONE ROMANTIC THRILLER:

ON THE EDGE

May 2023

***

COMING SOON:

QUINTESSENTIALLY (Stand-alone, small-town, second-chance, secret baby contemporary romance)

July 2022

ROYAL REFLECTIONS SERIES:

RILED REIGN (prequel)

September 2022

RUTHLESS REIGN

November 2022

STAND-ALONE ROMANTIC SUSPENSE:

SILVER LINING (Age-gap/ Older woman)

October 2022

***

READY TO BINGE:

SIN SERIES:

Prequel: WHITE RIBBON

August 2021

RED SIN

October 2021

GREEN ENVY

January 2022

GOLD LUST

April 2022

BLACK KNIGHT

June 2022

STAND-ALONE ROMANTIC SUSPENSE:

KINGDOM COME

November 2021

DEVIL'S SERIES (Duet):

Prequel: "FATES DEMAND"

Prequel - March 18

DEVIL'S DEAL

May 2021

ANGEL'S PROMISE

June 2021

WEB OF SIN:

SECRETS

October 2018

LIES

December 2018

PROMISES

January 2019

TANGLED WEB:

TWISTED

May 2019

OBSESSED

July 2019

BOUND

August 2019

WEB OF DESIRE:

SPARK

Jan. 14, 2020

FLAME

February 25, 2020

ASHES

April 7, 2020

DANGEROUS WEB:

Prequel: "Danger's First Kiss"

DUSK

November 2020

DARK

January 2021

DAWN

February 2021

* * *

THE INFIDELITY SERIES:

BETRAYAL

Book #1

October 2015

CUNNING

Book #2

January 2016

DECEPTION

Book #3

May 2016

ENTRAPMENT

Book #4

September 2016

FIDELITY

Book #5

January 2017

* * *

THE CONSEQUENCES SERIES:

CONSEQUENCES

(Book #1)

August 2011

TRUTH

(Book #2)

October 2012

CONVICTED

(Book #3)

October 2013

REVEALED

(Book #4)

Previously titled: Behind His Eyes Convicted: The Missing Years

June 2014

BEYOND THE CONSEQUENCES

(Book #5)

January 2015

RIPPLES (Consequences stand-alone)

October 2017

CONSEQUENCES COMPANION READS:

BEHIND HIS EYES-CONSEQUENCES

January 2014

BEHIND HIS EYES-TRUTH

March 2014

* * *

STAND ALONE MAFIA THRILLER:

PRICE OF HONOR

Available Now

* * *

THE LIGHT DUET:

Published through Thomas and Mercer Amazon exclusive

INTO THE LIGHT

June 2016

AWAY FROM THE DARK

October 2016

* * *

TALES FROM THE DARK SIDE SERIES:

INSIDIOUS

(All books in this series are stand-alone erotic thrillers)

Released October 2014

* * *

ALEATHA'S LIGHTER ONES:

PLUS ONE

Stand-alone fun, sexy romance

May 2017

ANOTHER ONE

Stand-alone fun, sexy romance

May 2018

ONE NIGHT

Stand-alone, sexy contemporary romance

September 2017

A SECRET ONE

April 2018

MY ALWAYS ONE

Stand-one, sexy friends to lovers contemporary romance

July 2021

QUINTESSENTIALLY

Stand-alone, small-town, second-chance, secret baby contemporary romance

July 2022

* * *

INDULGENCE SERIES:

UNEXPECTED

August 2018

UNCONVENTIONAL

January 2018

UNFORGETTABLE

October 2019

UNDENIABLE

August 2020

About the Author

ALEATHA ROMIG

Aleatha Romig is a New York Times, Wall Street Journal, and USA Today bestselling author who lives in Indiana, USA. She grew up in Mishawaka, graduated from Indiana University, and is currently living south of Indianapolis as well as part of the year in Bradenton, Florida, USA. Before she became a full-time author, she worked days as a dental hygienist and spent her nights writing. Now, when she's not imagining mind-blowing twists and turns, she likes to spend her time with her friends and family, including her beloved grandchildren.

Aleatha released her first novel, CONSEQUENCES, in August of 2011. CONSEQUENCES became a bestselling series with five novels and two companions released from 2011 through 2015. The compelling and epic story of Anthony and Claire Rawlings has graced more than half a million e-readers. Her next series, INFIDELITY (not about cheating) hit New York Times, Wall Street Journal, and USA Today best-seller lists. Aleatha has since released over thirty-five novels in multiple genres: dark romance, romantic suspense, thriller, and romantic comedy. She went back to her dark roots with the new trilogies of the Sparrow Webs: WEB OF SIN, TANGLED WEB, WEB OF DESIRE, and DANGEROUS WEB and the Devil's Series Duet: DEVIL'S DEAL and ANGEL'S PROMISE.

The titles keep coming. Be sure to check out her website to stay up to date.

Aleatha is a "Published Author's Network" member of the Romance Writers of America, NINC, and PEN America. She is represented by Kevan Lyon of Marsal Lyon Literary Agency and Wildfire Marketing.

Stay connected. Sign up for her newsletter and follow here:

Facebook / Twitter / TikTok / Instagram / Pinterest / Bookbub

Made in the USA
Las Vegas, NV
03 May 2022

48366138R00138